ISO KILLER

STEPHEN HARDING

DEDICATION

As ever, I'd like to dedicate this to all those people who've supported me on my ventures so far....You should still know who you are unless you've already been carted off in a white jacket.

There are various friends and colleagues who also appear in my books in various guises. I'm sorry if you don't last long, suffer some sort of agonising death or in some cases do quite well and sound very heroic. Just remember, you wanted to be in them.... but I love you all really.

I'd like to give a special thanks to all those who've been good enough to provide me with feedback on my writing, yet continuously ask for more.... May I suggest you seriously look at getting professional help, unless you're one of the above.....

Thanks to all of those in 'Jean's Café in Berrylands for being there, for the wonderful coffee and being such nice people.

My exceptional proof reader, Sarah James whose time and effort is much appreciated, so much more than she can ever imagine.

All the best to the real Liberty Rock who's doing well in the business world just as I knew she would. She's a cut above the rest.....

Finally, R.I.P. Peter Satterthwaite (We all miss you).

PROLOGUE

The child's eyelids blinked open and shut in quick succession before they felt brave enough to keep them fully open. They knew what had just happened had been as real as anything they'd ever experienced in their eight and a half years. Tears evolved from anguish and frustration welled up in the child's eyes as it gazed around at the carnage of the car crash it had been in, before it coughed heavily and felt a deep pain roar inside its chest. Everything around it seemed to be saturated in blood and the inside of the vehicle resembled a meat factory in which a mad butcher had gone on some kind of berserker rampage. There were moments of total confusion as the child's brain tried to make sense of the scene; both parents still firmly strapped in their seatbelts in the front of the car, both seemingly crushed from the impact. The youngster recalled the sound of metal scrapping against metal as the other car forced them from the road and straight into a tree. Not long had past, but it already seemed like it had happened ages ago.

STEPHEN HARDING

Suddenly, the child heard footsteps through the back window that it had opened sometime earlier in the journey and moments later, it noticed the figure of a tall man with long black hair and a scruffy beard came into view. He approached the back of the car, leant towards them and yanked the door wide open. The child thought it resembled the guy from the garage they'd stopped at to get petrol; the one the child's father had nearly knocked over when they'd set off again, but hadn't been paying proper attention. The child's father had shouted sorry, but the guy hadn't looked best pleased. But that was miles away from where they were right now.

The man reached across the child's body. The smell of stale alcohol invaded the youngster nostrils as he leaned over to unfasten their seat belt. For reasons it couldn't explain, the child associated the nauseating stench with evil. The reason soon became clear as the man wrenched the child from the car and cast them to the ground, not giving a single sign of compassion as he unzipped the fly on his jeans and pulled out his floppy penis and pissed all over the poor child, who lay helpless on the ground. Once he'd finished, shaken the drips off and zipped his fly, the man gazed down at the sodden, stinking, terrified figure. Clearly approaching the limits of fear induced shock, the child obviously needed help. The man simply stood and said a few short words that would be imprinted in its memory forever.

'I'm giving you a chance kid. I also wanted you to understand that I ain't going soft in my old age. It's a big fucked up world that we live in right now and there's no need to play by the rules any longer. Just take what you want and do whatever you wanna do. Don't let people ever take advantage of you anymore. Just make sure you get full payback on anyone who pisses you off or tries to humiliate you in any way. Life's too short kid, and that's something you'll find out for yourself one day.'

The man pulled a couple of things from his pocket and, as the child gazed up, it recognised the familiar clicking sound that it had heard whenever its dad had lit a cigarette. The kid watched as the man started to chuckle and casually lit a roll-up. The youngster's eyes widened in surprise as the scruffy man began to walk back towards the car. Just as it looked like he might help its trapped parents, the man flicked the burning cigarette in through the open back window, carried on walking to his own truck, got in and drove off into the distance.

The child struggled to its feet, knowing that it needed to get as far away as it could in case the vehicle exploded. Taking one last look at the car, the kid saw a movement and the shocking realisation that its mother was still alive hit it full on. Her scream as the car burst into flames and the desperation in her eyes would haunt the child's memory forever. Yet, it was the stranger's words that stayed etched in its mind and would repeat themselves each and every night in the week to come. As the petrol tank had caught, the force of the blast threw the youngster to the ground again. The next thing it remembered was waking up in a hospital bed, screaming for its mother.

CHAPTER 1

The pain was intense, like nothing he'd ever felt before. Everything was a blur, yet he knew that his body, especially his legs, were completely shattered having fallen from such a great height just moments before. There was also the matter of the stinging pain in his neck; he'd been jabbed with something unbelievably sharp by someone just before falling from the third floor. A large pool of blood surrounded the man and that was still busy expanding as he lay helpless, totally unable to move a single part of his body. The very essence of life was leaving the shattered frame as the blurred images of other shoppers continued to stare.

Jared Boyle, Operations Director of a very successful business, recalled the strange words the person in the hoodie had uttered just before pushing him over the balcony.

'I can assure you, you won't be upsetting any auditors ever again, you fucking arsehole.'

At only twenty-eight years old, and fit from regular workouts in the local gym, Jared was ever the fighter and tried to fight back hard at first. He enjoyed life and really didn't want to die without doing all the things he still had planned, especially with his girlfriend, who he adored and had hoped to spend the rest of his life with. Through some uncanny strength of willpower, although he lay all torn and twisted inside, Jared still managed to find enough strength to raise his head a tiny fraction, open his mouth and attempt to suck in a tiny portion of the precious air that encircled him. Sadly, this was to no avail, as seconds later the young man suffered another sharp stab of pain before his brain began to fog up from lack of oxygen. His thoughts grew weaker and weaker until they completely faded away. A terrifying darkness descended and Jared breathed no more.

As word spread like wildfire, just like vultures, the crowds continued to gather around. Before long, the morbid creatures were eventually ushered away by the shopping centre's security staff as the emergency services had finally arrived and started to cordon off the whole area.

*

'It's good to see you again,' Debbie said as she offered her hand and greeted her visitor. She opened the door to the reception and let the auditor in before asking him to sign the visitor's book, which lay open on the table nearest to them. With those steps fully completed, she handed him a visitors badge with a key fob that would allow him to walk around the building unaided if need be.

The auditor gave her a nice friendly smile. He reached

out to take the badge attached to a visitor's lanyard, placed it over his head and followed her to the board room where the opening meeting would eventually take place. Debbie informed him of the health and safety rules and the fact that there were no planned fire drills that day. She then left him to set up his laptop while she went to get him a cup of tea and inform the Managing Director he'd arrived and would be ready for the opening meeting within the next ten minutes. Debbie certainly felt under no great pressure as the auditor had conducted the previous audit in a manner that had been professional, informative and extremely helpful to the company, even pointing out ways they could improve the business, which was all part of the ISO9001:2015 Standard for their Quality Management System. She remembered it as a pleasant day at the time, and hoped this one would prove to be just as useful. There was however, one significant change. This time, she'd have to factor in a new Managing Director and this one was an entirely different beast from the previous one. He was not well liked by a large majority of the staff, but that was something he'd soon discover for himself.

Debbie Drinkwater had been born and raised in Lowestoft, Suffolk and still carried a slight accent which stood out in certain words she used. It wasn't something she noticed herself, yet every so often someone would pick up on it and tease her. She was short at five-foot-two, and although she wasn't what you'd class as one of the world's most beautiful women, there was still something quite attractive about her. It helped that she had one of the most wonderful smiles that proved quite infectious at times. She'd worked at the company for the last twelve years as the Office Manager and was pretty much part of the furniture. That was until Gerry Barnes had finally retired from his role as the head of the company.

When David Boston arrived to take his place, everything had pretty much changed overnight. Seeing the writing on the wall, some staff had left of their own accord, but many had also been laid off, with the new MD ensuring they left with nothing. He really wasn't a nice person, and Debbie wondered just how long it would take the auditor to realise.

*

It wasn't the easiest of things to do, but Liberty was fast learning how to come to terms with the new regime and adapt to her new way of life. Not that she'd had any other choice, other than to give up her job and independence. That was not something this lady had even wanted to consider; it just wasn't in her nature. The fact that she wasn't yet bent and broken, as she'd already seen happen to others who'd suffered a similar fate, helped a great deal and this gave her some hope for the future.

As Liberty Rock reached over and placed her coffee cup on the table beside her, she realised her hands were starting to shake. Just as the physio had told her to do every now and again in order to keep the blood flowing around her body, she reached out and attempted to stretch the muscles in her shoulders and arms. Just as it had a few times before, her left arm let out a loud clicking sound, but she knew that was something she'd just have to get used to. At least her upper limbs were responding, which was more than could be said for her useless bloody legs.

Liberty's mind drifted back to why she was confined to the damned wheelchair; she'd been shot by Paul Dunn, a would-be gangster from one of the local estates. She'd managed to link the area he'd lived in to a large number of drug dealing incidents and a couple of rape cases that had somehow fallen through the cracks. Following further investigation and a lot of police time and effort, they'd revealed a link to a whole series of irregularities. This had been part of one of the Specialist Evidence Recovery Imaging Services (SERIS) scams that some of her bent colleagues, Bob Langdon and his team had finally gone down for.

She'd first got involved with Paul Dunn or 'Dunny' as he was more commonly known, because he'd decided he had the god given right to just walk into a restaurant and attempt to abduct a young woman who was having a meal with a girlfriend. Going ballistic because the two women, aided by a member of staff and two other diners, had been brave enough to put up a fight, he'd brazenly pulled out a gun and waved it about before shouting he'd be back for revenge, adding that the others shouldn't have interfered.

At first, the case had been fairly straightforward, at least until Dunny had decided to target her and start a frustrating game of cat and mouse. Admittedly, he'd proved quite elusive and more of an adversary than she'd first expected.

It had been six months after the original incident that Liberty had stopped for a quick drink after work with a colleague in a bar located directly opposite the restaurant where the Paul Dunn incident had occurred. She hadn't even thought about it until she'd glanced across the street and spotted the man himself standing there as bold as brass, staring straight back at her with an insane grin on his face. Watching closely, she'd noticed a movement as he reached in and pulled something from inside his coat and pointed it in her direction. While her mind was busily trying to put two and two together and thinking the man was all mouth and no trousers, he'd casually walked towards her from across the road and fired.

Liberty remembered catching sight of a quick flash from the barrel of the gun and something shoot past her head at incredible speed. That was when her natural instinct to stay alive had kicked in and she'd automatically dived to the ground, badly spraining one of her shoulders in the process.

Only daring to gaze up once she felt she was stable enough, Liberty had seen Dunny standing over her a split second before the gun blazed again with a second bullet being fired towards her, but this time at a much closer range. The crazy bastard must have thought he'd killed her as he immediately turned and ran off, barging through the drinkers who couldn't believe what they'd just witnessed.

Fortunately for Liberty on that particular evening, a uniformed police officer by the name of Tommy Mason had been on duty, treading the beat of the local neighbourhood. As luck would have it, he'd entered the street just moments before and witnessed the whole thing. Tommy had been her absolute hero that evening, calling in the situation and asking for back-up assistance before chasing Dunny, who'd eventually managed to give him the slip and sliver off into the night like the snake he was. She recalled shouting out a warning to her colleague as she lay dazed and losing blood, but the rest of the evening seemed a complete blur until she'd eventually woken up in the hospital, feeling as if the whole world had finally managed to collapse in on her.

Still, that was then, and things had long since moved on in the four years since. Dunny had been caught and banged up for his misdoings, but Liberty had slowly grown more and more incapacitated. Her legs, feet and toes would suddenly take it in turns to go numb without any good reason, and that was getting more and more frequent as time went on. True to the nature of the woman, Liberty liked to believe she was indestructible and had done her best to ignore what was happening and carry on with the job she so loved. She didn't want to lose a single moment of time working on any of her cases, despite her partner Helen's constant assurance that she'd be perfectly fine handling things while her boss took a much-needed break, especially as she'd had so much outstanding leave to take at the time.

The real turning point had been when Liberty's legs had suddenly gone from under her when she and Helen had been out on a case. Helen didn't doubt for one second that her boss had been keeping quiet about the pain she was in, but she knew that this was something very serious indeed.

Like the trooper and close friend, she was, Helen had remained close by Liberty's side, holding her hand and talking to her as she tried her best to distract her while they waited patiently for an ambulance. Once it had finally turned up and the paramedics had quickly introduced themselves before springing into action, Helen started to explain the full story of what had happened. She stood back as her boss was loaded onto a stretcher and carefully placed inside the vehicle where they would carry out a series of further checks and tests on the way to the hospital.

That was the first time Helen had ever seen her boss cry; DCI Liberty Rock had always done a brilliant job of portraying herself as a hard-hitting cop who was never to be messed with, no matter what the circumstances were. Helen knew that was down to a combination of her tough upbringing and the harshness of trying to battle her way up the ever slippery, slidey ladder of the British police force. Yet she also knew Liberty had a warm heart and was a truly wonderful person deep down inside that armoured outer coating she always tried so hard to maintain.

*

The test results confirmed the bullet had moved and that it had been brushing up against her spinal cord for quite a while. Having been untreated for years and with Liberty not exactly taking things as easy as she'd been told, it had finally ruptured the cord and damaged most of the surrounding nerves.

Dr Jason, who'd been looking after Liberty from the moment she was first admitted to the hospital, had eventually told Liberty the hard truth: messages could no longer travel between her brain and her lower body and it was permanent. The outcome was that she was now paralysed from the waist down.

Naturally, Liberty was totally devastated and her mind retreated to its darkest recesses where nothing would be able to touch her. But Liberty was never one to give up and once the realisation that she'd be confined to a wheelchair for the rest of her life had sunk in, she'd battled hard to rise above the grief and misery of such a life changing experience. Mentally and physically she'd put in so much effort in to accept things and learn to adapt to her new way of life, so right now, DCI Liberty Rock was looking forward to getting back to work after such a long, tiresome break from what really made her tick.

*

Negotiating the lift had been easy enough, as had getting through the main door into the office. But despite all her preparation, on her first day back at work the central open-plan office was not proving quite as easy for Liberty to navigate in her wheelchair as she'd expected it to be. It was however, really great to be back in the mix. The place was alive and buzzing and she realised just how much she'd missed the atmosphere before spotting a few familiar faces from hers and other teams staring over at her. Warily negotiating her way through the heavy maze of chairs, desks and solidly constructed partitions that never gave way to anyone, hadn't been so easy either.

This whole area was loaded with colleagues from the Major Investigation Team (MIT), which formed one of the four command units of the Specialist Crime and Operation Directorate. They all greeted her and were genuinely pleased to see her back as she passed each of them by. Therefore, her plan to fly in under the radar and not have a big fuss made of her hadn't quite worked as far as she was concerned, and it certainly hadn't proved to be the plain sailing she'd expected.

With a bit more careful navigation, and some strategic reorganisation of the furniture, Liberty finally pulled up outside her boss's door and gave it a couple of hard taps. It was less than thirty-seconds before she heard the self-assured female voice on the other side calling for her to enter.

*

The audit had gone as well as could be expected. Debbie had proved to be a great host throughout the day. The only bit of trouble came when Mike had started to review one of the training, awareness and competency clauses.

During his time as MD, Gerry Barnes had been a firm believer in developing and nurturing his staff, backing this up with a decent budget that allowed them to grow and prosper within the business. David Boston on the other hand, had his own ideas on the subject which were completely at odds with his predecessor. He firmly believed that the real incentive for staff was simply to be able to keep their jobs if they worked hard enough. Any other incentives had completely disappeared, so staff had left in their droves.

It was very clear to Mike that this was a real risk to the business and, with Debbie unable to provide any records of training since David had taken charge; now meant Mike had no option but to raise the issue as a major finding. Mike told Debbie and, in turn, Debbie had informed David who immediately demanded to attend the closing meeting and challenge the decision.

David Boston raged at the auditor, believing he could simply bully the man into submission the same way he did the rest of his staff. Being experienced and well trained, Mike remained calm throughout. After a tough discussion, it was finally agreed that the major finding would stand and the company would need to present a suitable action plan, then provide evidence to demonstrate this had been done within the agreed timescale.

When the meeting had ended, Debbie showed Mike to the door and apologised for what had happened. She really liked the auditor and always felt he was fair, professional, and really knew his stuff whilst giving them some really useful advice. She also admired the way he'd stood up to her boss, but wondered if she'd be likely to see him again as she was starting her new job in three months' time. It seemed an awfully long time to wait before she could leave, but David had virtually forced all the existing managers to sign new contracts that worked in his favour. That was when the rot had really started to settle in and caused concerns to grow.

*

Mike Britton had driven back home along the A3 and was listening to London Grammar's latest work. The volume was turned up pretty loud as he negotiated the traffic which was steadily building up as people left work for the evening. The ever-amazing, beautiful sound of Hannah Reid's vocals swept over and through him and helped to calm him down as he thought back to how the closing meeting had gone with that aggressive prat of an MD. It was such a shame that one person could cause so much damage to a previously successful business. Mike felt incredibly sorry for the likes of Debbie Drinkwater and the other staff that he'd met and talked with that day. There was no doubting some of them would feel trapped there with mortgages to pay and families to support. Some could even be coming up to retirement and know only too well that getting a new job would be virtually impossible.

Sure enough, Hannah's charming voice worked its magic as Mike felt the tension gradually start to ease away as the back of his neck and shoulders began to loosen.

Mike flicked on the indicator and pulled into the small slip road often used as a rat run to avoid the busy traffic that built up on its way out of Kingston and the surrounding area. Placing his foot firmly on the accelerator to add a bit more speed, despite the road signs to the contrary, Mike approached a side road he needed to take with a little too much self-assurance. Just as he'd made the turn, he realised too late that he was going far too fast. His heart was in his mouth as the back of the car stepped and skidded on the recently tarmacked surface of the road.

Fortunately, with a good deal of driving experience behind him, Mike pulled it all together and managed to regain control. Calling himself a prat, he thanked his lucky stars there was nothing coming the other way before putting his foot down and flying down the next long street as it appeared before him.

Maybe this particular day had been marked the moment he'd decided to step out of bed. Mike had sensed it was one of those days that was likely to prove a bit difficult. Still, at least he'd have something to tell his three flatmates about that evening. They were a really good bunch and loved sharing stories, especially the ones they could look back on and laugh about over and over again. They often sat about and shared their stories. That was also one of the benefits of living with people you'd never met before.

CHAPTER 2

Detective Superintendent Heather Palmer had been busy sitting behind her desk with her mind caught up in all the red tape that inevitably came with her job. Once the door opened and she saw who was there, she immediately jumped to her feet. Heather, who was Liberty's boss, had been in charge of the Major Investigation Team (MIT), one of the four command units of the Specialist Crime and Operation Directorate, for the past eight years.

The MIT delves into murder, manslaughter and attempted murder where the evidence of intent was unambiguous, or where risk to life was certain. It also investigates missing persons or abductions where a life may have been, or could be taken. A few years back, there'd been a major incident involving the conviction of Bob Langdon and his bent colleagues from the SERIS team that proved to be quite devastating, although that particular investigation had also created a much greater understanding between her and DCI Liberty Rock, who'd started in the force with her at round about the same time. They'd since formed a very deep trust that would prove very hard to break, which was a rarity in the Force these days.

Just like Liberty, she'd worked her way up the ladder and fought hard to forge a reputation for herself as someone not to be messed with. At fifty-nine, Heather looked much younger than her years. She was tall, attractive, and extremely intelligent but didn't suffer fools gladly. She dressed for practicality rather than fashion, with no-nonsense suits and shoes made for walking in. Why any woman would want to put herself through the torture of high heels was a mystery to her, a subject that she and Liberty had discussed on more than one occasion over the years. Heather often wore her hair tied, which accentuated her high cheekbones and, along with her piercing dark eyes, helped her portray the tough image she wanted.

Just before the interruption, she'd been sat at her desk feeling a little annoyed at the ever-growing piles of papers in her in-tray that never seemed to get anywhere fast. She thought that working as a double agent to help bang up Langdon and his gang would have eased the weight on her somewhat, but all it seemed to have done was prove that she and her team were something to be reckoned with, for those both inside *and* outside the law. She'd had quite a bit of pressure from above over her decision not to retire Liberty early following her disability, yet she also knew they fully understood how brilliant a detective she was.

Liberty's experience was second to none. She was extremely valuable and an absolute godsend to the likes of her partner Helen, and that would remain the same for any other newbie's wanting to become good cops in the future. The force certainly needed more like her, and that in itself made keeping her on a no-brainer.

'I'm sorry Helen can't be here. I'm afraid I needed her to look at something else for me while I went through this with you. There's still a crazy amount of pressure coming down from above as you well know. The trouble is that it never ever seems to let up.' Heather handed the start of the case file to Liberty and then said 'Welcome back' officially. Here's something that's already looking like one of those nightmare jobs you always seemed to like so much. Why don't you start by getting your teeth into that one, Liberty? It will prove to me that I've made the right decision in bringing you back. As you can well imagine, the head honchos still have their doubts about you coming back, especially as there are all manner of HR and health and safety implications to deal with. I'm not even going to go into the financial costs and the difference of opinions that have gone to and fro, so let's just prove them all wrong shall we?' It was such a relief for Liberty to have someone like Heather looking out for her. Most other bosses in the force, many of who she'd come across in the past, would simply have stuck the knife in without flinching.

*

Emily Hart had been one of the first on the train. It felt just like any other day of the week as she entered the carriage alongside the commuters she travelled with each morning. As was her normal routine, she made her way over to her favourite spot and sat down in the first empty seat. It was a very busy route during the working week, other than in the school holidays, therefore you had to be fairly quick unless you wanted to stand for the whole journey. She'd just beaten a young businessman to the seat by the window, but he'd just walked off in a huff looking for somewhere else to sit. It was then that she'd taken a cursory glance at the man sat directly opposite her. She started to feel uneasy. It took her a moment to process what she'd just seen. She lifted her head to take a longer look, just to make sure she wasn't seeing things. Sure enough, the man had a very odd, but distinct look on his face. He had weird staring eyes and an extremely pale, sickly looking expression that was growing worse and worse with each passing second. Suddenly, almost as if it had been planned to happen that way, the train hit a sharp bend. That was what caused the man to fall forward and land head first, right in her lap.

Emily screamed loudly. It was more from shock than anything else as she realised, she now had what looked to be a dead body resting on her.

The two passengers she was sharing the four-seater section with sprang into action to help the stricken woman, who was still screaming. The man was a dead weight, but they managed to ease him back up into a sitting position and, thinking the man might have had a heart attack, called for help from anyone who had medical experience. The guard was summoned by one of the watching passengers and, thankfully no one had panicked and pulled the emergency alarm, which meant they'd be able to sort things out at the next station.

Emily had finally stopped screaming, but the poor woman was clearly in shock.

*

When Liberty eventually arrived back at her desk, she found Helen sitting with her feet up with her back towards the door. Her partner's mind seemed to be miles away. Helen was casually studying the picture board on the wall at the front of the room; her hands intertwined behind her head in her usual thinking pose.

Inspector Helen Morgan had originally been paired with Liberty to add to her skills. She'd been spotted as somebody who possessed exemplary abilities that would slot well into the unit and make up any shortfalls. But she'd also been partnered with DCI Liberty Rock so that she could keep an eye on her for Heather, who was worried about Liberty's less than conventional style in the politically correct world of policing. There had been a bit of friction between them at first, but after taking down two deadly serial killers, who'd given them a much harder time than they'd ever have bargained for, this had turned into a proper trust and friendship.

Helen was mixed race with short, black curly hair that perfectly suited her facial features. The low-cut blouse's and short skirts she'd worn when they'd first met four years ago had been replaced by stylish business suits that were both classy and practical.

Where Liberty was single and coming up to retirement, Helen was twenty-nine and living with fellow officer Mark Bentley. Mark had worked in SERIS, the unit that had been torn apart when the scam they'd been running for years had finally been uncovered and the body of Emma Still, who had been raped and murdered by the brutal group of bent cops, was discovered dumped alongside Mark's in a remote wooded area.

Mark had been lured into a trap and tortured for helping Liberty and Helen in their quest to incriminate the team. He had been left for dead beside Emma, but had miraculously survived and days later been found barely alive. Liberty knew the scars were still there, deep inside the man, and that he'd never be able to forget such an ordeal.

'There's something in these picture's that's really starting to bug me.' Helen declared, once she'd realised Liberty was back and sitting behind her.

'I'll suss it eventually, but it's bloody annoying right now. I just can't seem to put my finger on It.' Liberty trusted her partner and knew that when her hunch revealed itself, it could well be worth following up on. Liberty's desk had been changed for one that went up and down at the flick of a button. This was all part of the new Agile Workspace Plan that the force was running as a pilot scheme in selected stations. It was aimed at encouraging people to stand more, especially those with bad backs. Being able to stand at her desk was bugger all use to Liberty, but it did mean she could raise it to the correct height for her wheelchair. They'd also been kind enough to install one in her flat, which was truly remarkable and meant she could work from home whenever she wanted to.

*

Mark Bentley had been off work for a long time because of his injuries. On his return, he'd been asked to help get SERIS back up and running the way it should always have run. He'd done a brilliant job and impressed the right people along the way. His reward for all his hard work and dedication was to gain a decent promotion. He and Helen had now been together for four years and although he'd have liked to be engaged to her, he knew it was still a taboo subject. He knew he was a lucky man to have her in his life and he didn't want to rock the boat, but secretly he was struggling with the fact that her job was demanding and came first ninety-nine percent of the time. Even having Helen for that one percent would have been fine under any normal conditions.

Over the years, Mark had noticed their lovemaking would step up a few gears whenever one of Helen's cases was about to reach its peak. The adrenaline rush from her work heightening her awareness and keeping her on tenterhooks seemed to be an addiction and would get him equally excited. But even that was suffering lately, as Mark had started to grow more and more depressed. The trouble was he couldn't work out if that was because of what he'd been through, the pressures of the job, or a combination of everything. Whatever it was, it needed to be sorted out soon; otherwise things were going to go rapidly downhill.

*

Mike Britton was in his early thirties and already divorced. On reflection, he'd married far too young. But all his mates had done the same. It wasn't cool to be single in that world and he didn't buck the trend back then, but now he was older and wiser, Mike felt he was a completely different person now.

He was of medium build with short black hair. His face was round with average sized features. In fact, everything about the way he looked was average. Being newly single had made him want to relive his youth, which was partly why he was now shacked up with three housemates in a large rented house in suburban Surrey. He had a room to himself on the ground floor, which wasn't exactly massive, but that suited him just fine for now. If asked, Mike would happily admit he was slightly jealous of Malik who lived up in the loft with the bonus of access to a small roof terrace, although it probably wasn't quite as safe as it should have been. They'd sent numerous letters to the landlord about the guardrail on many occasions, but still nothing had been done about it, which was very piss poor in his eyes.

Malik was an IT freak who preferred to have his own space. He could be very weird at times, but also very sociable when he wanted to be. He was originally from Egypt, or somewhere thereabouts, and worked from home designing websites. Most of it went right over Mike's head in all honesty. Malik did quite well from what Mike could make out, and he always paid his share of the rent when due. Mike's other two flatmates, Jenny and Tom, were the complete opposite. They were party people who lived in what Mike called *The Hippy World* where love, drink and drugs were, according to them, *'the only way to go'*. Although he was pleased that in reality drugs were much further down the list, with both tending to prefer the first two a whole lot more. Mike was easily led by Jenny, who was moody at times but really flirty when she was in the right frame of mind. There was no denying she had a really fit body with legs that seemed to go on forever, which Mike couldn't help but notice, especially when she wore sexy clothing that showed them off in a quite spectacular way. Jenny knew that many men would want to fuck her, and she'd use her charms, going out of her way to tease and get what she wanted, whenever she wanted. She'd often flash her knickers, spread her legs open when she knew that Mike or Malik were looking in her direction and even go commando at times, which was even worse. She knew she could send the pair of them wild at times, even bring them to the point where they'd end up in the bathroom jerking off. That meant Tom was either absolutely oblivious to what was going on, or he was having a laugh at their expense.

Despite their differences, they'd bonded and worked really well as housemates, taking it in turns to cook and do the chores. They'd a set a rota in place, but were more than happy to swap things around at times, especially when Mike had to be away, which he needed to do every now and again as part of his job. One thing they all loved were Mike's stories about some of the companies he visited and how different they were across the industries he audited. They all admired the way he handled things, particularly when it came to some of the more awkward customers. The other three didn't know how they'd have approached these situations, and they certainly wouldn't have been as diplomatic as Mike. Everything Mike told them was in strictest confidence, and therefore they'd all agreed to follow a vow of silence, which he hoped and prayed they'd always respect. There was an auditor's code of conduct and he'd signed all sorts of terms and conditions when he'd joined the company. But as far as he was concerned, these three were his family for now, so in his mind he wasn't really breaking any rules.

*

As agreed, Liberty and Helen stopped off at Jean's Café on their way home. It was their favourite coffee shop, located in a part of Berrylands, just up the hill from the middle of Surbiton. Zoe and Daisy were busy running the place that day and although it was nearly closing time, they knew Zoe was pretty laid back with her regulars and they'd still have plenty of time to chat. The only other people in the place were Dave and his huge dog Reggie, alongside Raymond and his little dog Odie, who looked miniscule up against Dave's. Liberty asked after Sarah, Zoe's mum who she really liked, and Alexandra, who also worked there on alternate days but was said to be leaving sometime soon. She then turned her attention back to Helen.

'What are you thinking?' she asked. Helen looked over and placed her cup carefully back down on the saucer before responding.

'You know those gut-feeling moments when you're sure something's linked but can't quite put your finger on it Lib's?' One look into Helen's eyes told Liberty that her partner was troubled.

'Well there are two cases that I've been looking at just recently that keep coming back at me and are playing silly buggers inside my head. I haven't had much luck with either of them so far, but I'm pretty sure they're connected.'

There was a bit of a pause as Reggie decided to get up and walk past their table with Dave shouting for him to come back and sit down. Reggie wasn't the sort of dog anyone could ignore; as his size was impressive, but he wouldn't harm a fly and was actually rather shy.

'I know one's the death of that young man at the shopping centre the other day because that's one of the ones that Heather passed over recently, and one of the photograph's I've noticed you've been so busy with. I'm not sure what the other one is, but what's the connection?' Liberty asked her partner, who was getting increasingly irritable about the whole damned thing.

Liberty knew the feeling well, as she'd been in the same boat and spent endless time going over cases in her head at night and looking worse for wear for it the next day. Helen already had a few dark rings under her eyes, despite her attempt to hide them with make-up, and that was really unlike her. The tables were definitely starting to turn and Helen was becoming the type of person that Liberty used to be. In all honesty, despite no longer having the use of her legs thanks to some prize dickhead with a gun, she was still like it.

Helen took a quick swig of her coffee before finally answering. Helen didn't want to make a fool of herself, but Liberty was both her boss and a friend who was genuinely interested in anything she had to say.

'Well there was that incident on a train last week where a businessman was found dead in one of the carriages.' Helen looked across to see if there was any sign of reaction from Liberty, but nothing was forthcoming, so she decided to carry on.

'It turned out that the deceased, who they originally thought was having a heart attack, had in fact been injected in the neck with a drug called succinylcholine chloride, which can prove fatal. That particular case is currently sitting with another MIT, which is probably the reason you're not aware of it, but I'm wondering if Heather will let us look into it a bit further, seeing as it comes under her jurisdiction?' Helen knew there used to be over thirty Major Investigation Team's operating in London with just under a thousand police officers, two hundred civilian staff, and fourteen senior detectives working in them; but, just like many other business that had gone through restructures and budgetary issues, changes had taken place. Heather's Command Unit was now one of six, with the five other MIT's consisting of around fifty staff.

Liberty put her hand on Helen's shoulder in a gesture of support and told her that she'd be more than happy to talk to Heather.

'If you don't ask, you don't get in this world,' she said, but her mind had already started its process of shifting methodically through what her partner had just told her. Draining the last of their cappuccinos, the two female detectives promptly grabbed their belongings from the table then bade good evening to everyone before leaving. Zoe had already turned the sign on the door to CLOSED, picked up the empty coffee cups and took them around the back of the counter to wash them as Dave grabbed Reggie's collar and got up from his favourite spot on the sofa.

CHAPTER 3

They'd all had a lot to drink at the pub; it was a Friday night and that was when they started to relax. Everyone had agreed it had been a long week, but they'd left the pub together and were now back at their place and ready for more. Malik, as expected, had been a party pooper and headed off to his bed, despite protests that the night was still young. That left Mike, Jenny and Tom to crash out in the living room. Mike headed for one of the three bean bags while the other two settled down on the large blue sofa with its fake leopard skin throw. They opened the three bottles of beer that they'd fished out of the fridge before getting comfortable. Tom was the first to speak.

'You know that Boston guy you talked about in the pub? The one who was the Managing Director of that company and argued with you at the end? What a wanker he sounded.' Tom grabbed his beer bottle and took a good, long swig before carrying on with his rant.

'I really hate it when some dickhead like that joins a

perfectly good company and is given the power to pretty much rip it apart. And in such a short space of time too. I had a boss a few years back who sounds very similar, but he ended up by being found dead in a river. I don't think they ever discovered who did it or why it happened. You remember that don't you Jen? We'd only been going out together for a couple of months. It seems such a long time ago now.'

Jenny simply smiled and gulped back a mouthful of lager.

'Malik made it quite clear that he can't stand those sorts of characters either. But it sounds like that Debbie woman you mentioned won't be there if you ever go back to audit that place again,' Tom added, having obviously not listened to the bit about the fact that she was already getting ready to leave.

Mike was trying his best to listen, but he couldn't concentrate all that well as Jenny was up to one of her teasing games. The strapless dress she wore didn't really help; it clung to her body like a second skin and accentuated her figure highlighting her pert nipples and confirming she wasn't wearing a bra.

As usual, Jenny's makeup was subtle, but just enough to accentuate her long black eyelashes, and her *come to bed* eyes that some men found hard to refuse. Her straight, long black hair hung free over her shoulders and stretched down her back. It seemed to have a life of its own when she leant forward to grab up her drink, giving her a certain wild, untamed look that accentuated the beauty that radiated from every single pore of her body. Tom knew Mike had the hots for his girlfriend, but he'd always made out that it wasn't a problem. He really liked the guy, and as he and Jen had a pretty open relationship and an understanding about free love that harked back to the good old hippy era, he wasn't all that concerned about her flirting and had made that clear to Mike and even Malik in the past.

If he was forced to admit it, Tom actually enjoyed it when Jenny dressed up in her sexy gear and teased people by acting all provocatively. He knew she loved to tease Mike by parting her legs and licking her lips just to get him going and see if she could give him a stiffy. This was a woman who was well aware of her sexuality and very confident she could get what she wanted, just as long as she was in the right sort of mood.

*

Liberty was already a dab hand at driving the large black Sirus Automatic Volkswagen Caddy that had been tailored to her needs. Thanks to all of Heather's hard work and her refusal to back-down with the finance bods, it had a powered tailgate, automatic foldout ramp and a boot that opened remotely. It was known as a Wheelchair Access Vehicle or WAV for short, and meant she could drive her wheelchair in from the back and slot her chair into the driver's position without any help. The whole thing worked brilliantly, it hadn't taken long to get used to and it gave her total autonomy.

Having arrived home and wheeled her way up the ramp without needing to use the railing, Liberty realised she'd already come a long way in learning to deal with her disability. But her muscles had been put through their paces during the day and her arms and shoulders ached.

She headed for the kitchen to make a cup of coffee

and gulp down two painkillers. Everything had been designed for her to reach things easily, and for this she was truly grateful to the force for supporting her so well. She knew much of that had been down to Heather and her insistence on keeping her on as a DCI. There had also been talk about getting her a powered wheelchair, which could perform all sorts of miracles, including allowing her to move up and down to reach things more easily.

According to a rumour she'd heard on the station grapevine, it was on order, but it was a secret so she'd have to act surprised if it ever appeared.

With the caffeine hit zipping around inside her and the painkillers doing their business, Liberty wheeled her way towards the bedroom, slowly took off her work clothes and covered herself with the fluffiest, most comfortable dressing gown she'd ever owned. Mark and Helen had given it to her as a *thank you for all your help,* and a *get well soon* present. It was sad that Mark's ordeal had made him much moodier, and Liberty knew that Helen was finding it tough.

Positioning her wheelchair at her desk just the way she liked it, Liberty read through the case file that Heather had handed her, which happened to be one of the ones Helen had been talking about in the coffee shop. She cast her eye over two well-thumbed photographs of Jared Boyle and read through his profile a couple of times. Suddenly, her years of experience and gut instinct kicked in. Jared just didn't seem like someone who would jump to his death in a shopping centre. There were far too many unanswered questions. A quick phone call to Helen and a few e-mails later, Liberty sat back to give herself a bit of head space.

'Hopefully tomorrow's visit to Tim Mears, the pathologist, will provide some answers,' she thought.

*

'Okay, I'm off to bed. So, you two have a good time,' Tom told them, as he headed off up the stairs. Mike looked at Jenny to gauge her reaction. She looked amazing and she knew it. Once the door had shut, she played with him for a while, giving him the sexiest looks she could muster.

From his seat on the beanbag, Mike's head was dead level with her knees. Following his line of sight, and knowing exactly where his gaze was fixed, Jenny gradually moved them apart to give him a proper view right up to the top of her legs. She knew he'd be fixated by the thong she was wearing, which didn't leave much to the imagination.

'The coast is clear Mikey boy. If you like what you see, there's a whole lot more. Why don't we have some fun?' she asked, as she lifted the front of her skirt and started to stroke the top of the bottle against the front of her thong. Mike didn't need any further coaxing and moved closer to the sofa with the front of his trousers bulging.

Jenny leaned over and placing the bottle back down on the table, their faces now drew level. Mike moved towards her and they started to kiss. They were gentle with each other at first, but things soon heated up. Jenny was going for it with real meaning as Mike pulled back just to double check she was OK with everything.

'How will Tom feel about this?' he asked.

'He'll be fine,' she'd fired back, before smothering his

mouth with hers so that he couldn't say anything else. They continued to kiss as Mike's hands explored the contours of her body, soaking up every single moment. He tweaked her pert nipples a few times through the flimsy material of her dress, while her right hand rubbed against his hard cock which was desperately aching to get free of his trousers. Yet Mike still took his time as he kissed her deeply on the lips then slowly moved his way to her beautiful neck, lightly nibbling towards her right ear and taking her ear lobe into his mouth.

Jenny started to breathe heavily. Tom was never as passionate as this. He preferred a fast fuck most of the time, although that had its own rewards, especially in public places where the chances of being caught simply added to the thrill.

Jenny reached up and tugged the top of her dress down to expose her breasts. Mike continued kissing and licking her neck, slowly working his way down to brush the tips of her nipples with his tongue. She let out a deep breath followed by a low sensual moan. Mike lips engulfed her swollen nipples one by one as she encouraged him to suck on them even harder. Jenny worked his trousers down and stroked his long cock. She spread her legs a little bit more and moved her hips forward to allow an easier entrance. Mike could feel the heat and wetness coming from her and allowed her hand to guide him inside her. Moving his hips forward to apply more pressure, Mike was about halfway in before he started to slowly pull out, then gently work his way back in again, and loving the feel of her black pubic hairs as they rubbed against his. Jenny pulled him towards her, urging him to plunge deeper and deeper inside her, grinding her hips into Mike's until a joined-up rhythm was set and then going full pelt.

Caught up in the moment with an animal-like aggression coursing through their minds and bodies, the sex between them was truly amazing.

They lay together on the sofa like lovers, but after two more sessions they called time and shuffled off to their respective bedrooms. Mike was sore but he knew he would sleep like a baby.

Jenny Manson was everything, and more than he ever thought she'd be. What just happened had confirmed to him that she was sexy, all woman and slightly mental with it.

He hoped there'd be a repeat performance in the near future. He was already up for it.

*

Liberty lay face up on her bed, the wheelchair parked right beside it; she'd already learnt her lesson about not being able to reach it properly.

Darkness was squeezing in around her. It felt strangely imposing as she lay in an awkward, tangled mess, the bed sheets crumpled up around her. The DCI could feel her heart thumping wildly in her chest. Her senses all seemed to be heightened for some bizarre reason. In some ways it felt quite thrilling, but was a little too scary for her liking. She knew it was partly a throwback to four years ago when she'd lost her sister and best friend to the serial killers who'd ripped her whole world apart. Liberty had suffered nightmares even before that, but these were worse. Yet strangely, they also kept her going and were the drivers that helped motivate her to rid the world of such sadistic killers, along with the rapists who believed they had a God-given right to do whatever they wanted, whenever they wanted, and then expected to get away with it. It was only cops like her and her colleagues who, despite the huge personal effect it had on their own private lives, still dedicated their time to put a stop to it.

So, Liberty had a pretty restless night, just as she always did. Each and every case, including some from the past, would float around in her mind, her thought processes reviewing her findings, deconstructing them so that she could piece them back together. It wasn't always a bad thing. Sometimes it would send her mind racing in all sorts of different directions, giving her fresh ideas. Sometimes it worked and sometimes it didn't. But whatever the outcome, Liberty's body had now become accustomed to the pattern of sleep deprivation and functioned pretty well under the circumstances.

CHAPTER 4

She removed her knickers, as that was all she usually slept in. Liberty hated pyjamas with a vengeance as they were far too restrictive and fiddly, plus she'd always slept that way even before her legs had decided to pack up. With much less difficulty than she used to, Liberty manoeuvred herself back into her faithful wheelchair. Once seated, she moved into the corridor and headed for the wet room where she eased herself over and onto the plastic seat before turning the shower on. It took a few minutes, but Liberty completely relaxed as the water beat down and allowed the tensions in her body and mind to lighten a little. Washing herself from top down, Liberty sat but still found it difficult to deal with the fact there was no feeling in her legs. There were the odd occasions when she thought she felt something, but that was more down to wishful thinking on her part. Soaping under the hot water enabled her to feel as if she were washing away the demons from the previous day and sort of allowed her to get her thoughts back where they needed to be. Being able to think straight was definitely one of the requisites for a DCI.

Heather had recently given her two newbies to bring into the team. One was Cheryl Burgess, a bright young lady who'd demonstrated the perfect attitude from the moment they met. But then there was Luke King, who she wasn't quite so sure about. He still seemed a little immature in some respects, but she still needed to give him a fair crack of the whip and not discriminate between the two of them. It was still a bit too early to tell how they'd get on, but once they'd been with her department for a while, things would definitely change. She knew she'd need to spend a bit of time with each of them to see how they performed, but it was also a matter of whether or not her workload would allow her that luxury.

With the water still beating down, Liberty sensed some of the tiredness had already gone away. Then, gritting her teeth and twisting the dial to a much colder setting, this really woke her up, as she gave out a little scream, despite knowing what would happen. Reaching over and wrapping the towel around her shoulders once she'd dried her lower half, which wasn't the simplest of things to do; Liberty set a smaller one on the seat of her wheelchair then carefully transferred her body across. Wheeling back into the bedroom, she eased herself onto the bed and then began the daily struggle of getting her clothes on. This was also partly down to her stubbornness in refusing to have any help in the house since deciding she was quite capable of managing on her own.

Throwing on a bit of make-up, Liberty finally returned the two wet towels to hang drying over the radiator before wheeling herself into the kitchen where she prepared tea and toast with a generous helping of rhubarb and ginger marmalade slapped on top.

Not long after, she was soon heading off to work and looking forward to seeing Tim Mears, who she'd known for a long, long time. She had a good working banter with the man, but was never about to admit she'd missed him. He now referred to her as 'Liberside' based on a popular TV show from the early seventies that had starred the actor Raymond Burr. In the programme he worked as a consultant for the San Francisco police force solving all kinds of murders each week, which was so far removed from reality.

His character had been shot on vacation and paralysed from the waist down before being confined to a wheelchair. Liberty even had a photograph of him on her bedside table that Helen and Mark had given her when she'd been worried about her future. Apart from that, Tim was one of the few other people who could get away with such things, yet she'd usually manage to come up with something to get her own back when he did.

*

For what seemed a bit of a gap in the way things were going just lately, this was what Mike would have classed as a decent week as far as his auditing role went. He'd had two jobs in Berkshire and one in Kent, and was now finishing another one off at four-thirty on a Thursday afternoon. Thankfully, this job was much closer to home and based in one of those managed office buildings that was fine if the landlord was a decent type and not just after the tenant's money.

Friday was an administration day that would allow him to catch up on report writing and preparation for the next week's work, which suited him perfectly. In the meantime, his mind had shot back to his session with Jenny on the sofa last week. This had happened quite a few times, but those thoughts would simply have to go on hold as the Quality Manager, Sharon Higson and her Financial Director boss, Daniel Rosser now sat before him for the closing meeting with their pens poised and ready. Having run through the mandatory requirements and explained what had been covered during the audit with only two minor non-conformances having been raised, Mike was completely caught off guard when Daniel suddenly turned and started to raise his voice at Sharon, who subsequently burst into tears. Apparently, her bonus was based on her not having any findings raised. Therefore, with such an antiquated regime in place, in Daniel's eyes she had basically failed and needed to be the one who'd be answerable for such actions. Mike immediately jumped to her defence and was quick to explain that for the size of the company and the activities they performed, these findings were in fact very low risk to the business. Without trying to be seen as having stepped out of line in any way, Mike then suggested that the bonus could prove better off it was based on Sharon identifying the root causes and then closing them out within the agreed timescales instead. He also emphasised the fact that this could also be classed as a possible improvement to the existing system if they either considered or fully approved the changes. Daniel was quite rude at that point and it all became quite embarrassing. Obviously, Mike could do no more as he remained calm then went on to explain about the report being sent electronically before thanking them for their hospitality while Sharon dried her eyes.

Eventually, Daniel stood up and left the room without saying another word or bothering to shake hands, while Sharon busily collected herself then escorted Mike back down to the reception area. She was clearly a lot more upset than she looked at that point in time, but she took back his visitor's badge with the best smile she could muster, and asked if he could please sign out.

Mike was glad that she'd thanked him for stepping in, but he knew only too well that she was the one who'd have to go back and face the consequences. There was no way that Daniel Rosser was going to change things, but the fact that Sharon had told him, 'Now you can see why he's known to everyone as Rosser the Tosser,' had really made Mike laugh as he finally drove out of the visitor's bay and set off on the main road back towards his home.

*

Liberty and Helen finally arrived at the hospital in the comfort of the big black VW Caddy and being well used to the routine; Helen stood back and waited as her boss manoeuvred the wheelchair out of the vehicle in a pretty impressive time. She knew full well that she'd be better off not offering to help, and she'd only ever made that mistake the one time. Once inside, they both signed in with the old jobsworth security guard being so much nicer to them than he ever used to be. It turned out that his wife also happened to be wheelchair bound, so they'd both assumed that that was what had caused him to be so grumpy in the first place. They gradually made their way along the familiar route to Tim's office, where he'd already agreed to meet them and run through a few things they'd needed. He looked surprisingly decent for a change, which was a little bit disconcerting to tell the truth. The guy physically stood before them in person without his overalls, rubberised apron and latex gloves needing to be worn for a change.

'Hi Tim,' they'd greeted the madcap pathologist almost simultaneously as they'd entered and stared in wonder, with Liberty finding it incredibly hard to recall the last time she'd ever seen him looking that way. Almost as if he could read their minds, and in answer to the question that was so busy burning away in both women's heads, Tim explained that he was making a stand and it was about time his colleagues did some work for a change, which only raised another question as to what had happened.

As luck would have it, the whole place had literally been refurbished within the last two years and been designed with disabled access in mind. This therefore allowed Liberty to move around a lot easier, which was more than could be said for most of the places they came across. Helen was well aware the two people she shared the room with loved nothing more than to wind each other up whenever they had a chance, and it wasn't long before Tim referred to her boss as 'Liberside' with her responding by calling him 'The Butcher.'

'Believe it or not, I was actually prepared for you both this morning. I've pulled the report on that Boyle guy you asked about and remember the autopsy quite well. We found traces of succinylcholine chloride in the blood, which is also referred to a Sux by certain people both in and out of the profession. It's worth noting that this drug is completely odourless, and it's even been described as a perfect poison for murder in the past, as well as having been used by a whole host of criminals around the world. In this case, it had been injected via the neck and would have caused almost immediate paralysis, although that would normally only last for about ten minutes before the body would try it's best to recover. Whoever did this, almost certainly knew what was likely to happen. The poor guy didn't stand a chance. Worst of all, he would have been fully aware of his plight when dropping the distance covered before splattering on the ground with nothing whatsoever to protect him. As expected, that was what killed him in the end. That was also confirmed by the large amount of damage we found to his internal organs along with the considerable extent of haemorrhaging that had occurred. If this matches up to the one you're trying to get for that guy on the train, I'd say you two have got another nasty piece of work running around out there that needs to be banged up good and proper.' It turned out that Helen had been correct in her belief about it not being suicide, but she still decided to keep her mouth shut for the time being.

'Well, what more can I add, apart from thanking you and saying that it's been a pleasure as always Timothy.' Liberty added, with a cheeky smile on her face.

'I must say that it surprises me you wanted to meet on this rather than just do this over the phone. Was there any particular reason for that, or is it that you're both so caught up in my amazing charm offensive that you find it incredibly hard to stay away?' Both women looked at each other and couldn't help but laugh out loud.

'I guess you've finally sussed us out.' Helen spoke up. 'We just can't get enough of you to be honest.' Then it was Tim's turn to smile, before he gazed down at Liberty and gave her his own personal view.

'I can see this one's already been hanging around you for far too long. Having one of you on my case was bad enough, but now I'm faced with the Terrible Twosome. God only knows how that's going to pan out.' As always, Tim offered to take them for lunch if they hung around for another half hour. Yet just as expected, they gently declined the offer as they now had to get on and find out a whole lot more, with both women chomping at the bit.

*

Liberty had dealt with Detective Inspector Dave Light in the past when he'd been busy covering the discovery of the body of the businessman who'd later been identified as John Wilson over at Waterloo. That was something she'd much rather have forgotten if she'd been given the choice, but unfortunately it was part of the serial killings by the same two evil creatures that had murdered both her sister and best friend during their evil reign of terror. Naturally, and as promised, she'd kept Dave informed and remembered not needing to take up the offer of assistance he'd so kindly offered, although she had reciprocated at the time by providing him with something he'd been after for a good long while. Sometimes it was almost definitely a case of: 'If you scratch my back, I'll scratch yours'. The man had always remained very professional and come across as having a similar mindset to hers, which Liberty always found attractive and was more than happy to work with such people. There also tended to be a way of cutting out some of the unnecessary bullshit that included a lot of red tape, before getting straight to the crux of the matter. That was another reason she loved working so much with Heather and Helen a lot of the time. She fully understood the fact that her boss still had to jump through a shitload of hoops, yet she also kept much of that separate from her fellow workers and never seemed to complain. Switching her thoughts back to the subject in question, Liberty realised she was quite looking forward to meeting up with DI Dave Light again, especially if he could shed any further light on the subject. She laughed inwardly at the pun that was readily available, but didn't venture any further with the vast selection of crappy one-liners she knew Mark would have fired off without any hesitation at all.

Liberty knew for a fact that Mark was a bit of a concern for Helen right now. Her partner's boyfriend had never been the same after such a horrific ordeal, having been tortured and then left for dead by Bob Langdon's brainless cronies. He'd certainly lost the mojo he used to have, based on what she could make out when observing him. Still, with a bit of luck, a hope and a prayer, that would eventually sort itself out, although that was more a matter of time along with the man himself having to come to terms with things, and then putting the past to bed, once and for all.

Liberty couldn't quite understand why she seemed to be so distracted with her mind racing all over the place and not allowing her to focus properly. It really wasn't like her at all. Next up, she wondered if she could wangle a coffee or even lunch out of DI Dave Light, and because that was so unlike her, she seriously wondered if she was finally losing her marbles.

*

Mike had already found time to sit and prepare for the systems audit for the design company a few days earlier. He'd even spoken to Lorraine Carey, the companies' Quality Manager over the phone to double check they were ready for his visit. He'd needed to ensure that the right ISO Standard was being audited as the company were registered to more than one, plus he'd also wanted to check on the parking situation and any other areas he may have needed to know about. Mike found this usually paid off, especially for companies' such as this, where he'd never been to them before.

There were quite a few security conscious companies' he'd come across that wouldn't even let you in the building unless you had some form of ID such as a driving license or passport with you. Lorraine had sounded quite put out about the fact that he'd phoned her, so Mike was not surprised that the actual day of the audit day turned out to be a bit of a nightmare from the moment he stepped inside the door. Lorraine Carey turned out to be one of the rudest people he'd ever met in all his years as an auditor. She continually complained about how she had so little time, wore so many hats in the company and how under resourced they were with so many orders coming in all the time. Mike had initially tried all sorts of different approaches with a bit of humour, sympathy and even by providing a smattering of advice on how other companies tackled such issues. Sadly, it was to no avail, and no matter how hard he tried, the woman was almost impossible to get on with. Where he'd raised one major non-conformance and four minors on the company over the course of the day, Lorraine had gone absolutely ballistic each time he'd stopped to discuss and explain the reasons why. At one point, she'd even threatened to show him off the premises, but fortunately the Operations Manager had stepped in and managed to calm her down.

On one occasion, when Mike and this manager were sitting in the meeting room alone, as Lorraine had needed to rush off and answer a query with a customer over the phone, the man had apologised for her being so discourteous. He admitted that he and most of the other staff couldn't wait for her to leave the company, which was wishful thinking on their part, yet they all lived in hope.

*

To say the day had been a bad one would have been an understatement, and it didn't help that Mike got stuck in an awful traffic jam on his way back home. It appeared there'd been some sort of collision between a lorry and a car on one of the main junctions going southbound. That was what had caused the gridlock with loads of crazy tailbacks happening, even on the shortcuts he knew about, whilst attempting and failing to use some of the side streets.

Tom and Jenny were in the kitchen busily knocking up something to eat when he finally arrived home all wound up and feeling frustrated. He stopped to talk then told them about his crappy day and the evil woman he'd met while putting together a sandwich and a cup of tea as he was still too pissed off to cook anything for himself. During that time, Jenny had deliberately placed her hand on Mike's crotch and rubbed it up and down to tease him. Tom in the meantime, simply had his head turned towards the cooker and just carried on with the cooking as if nothing was happening. He knew from experience that it was best to let her play her little games if she wished to do so. Jenny could turn quite vicious if she didn't always get her own way.

'Maybe things will get better now that your home.' She whispered seductively, right up close in his ear.

Even the warmth of her breath and the closeness of her mouth had sent shivers up him and almost given him an instant hard-on. How could this woman be such a temptress all the time, and what was it about her that could do this to him? Grabbing up his food and drink from the work surface, Mike instantly left the kitchen and headed for his room. Mike knew he wouldn't have been able to be responsible for his actions if she'd carried on any longer and let her have her way. Tom, despite being a bit of a prat at times, was still a very nice guy who he had no intention of upsetting at all. Yet he really needed to have a word with his girlfriend about her behaviour at times. There was absolutely no way that he hadn't known what she was doing behind his back just then.

As Mike settled down and started to watch the news headline on the portable TV he had in his room up on the makeshift cupboard he'd never quite finished painting, he couldn't help but wonder if Jenny would be likely to make an appearance later and want to carry on where she'd left off. She knew exactly how Mike's mind worked, and the woman definitely had the genes of a nymphomaniac working away deep inside her. The woman was bloody well insatiable; no wonder she liked living in a house with other flatmates. Maybe his feelings about upsetting Tom would just have to go on hold for a while.

CHAPTER 5

Holmes House located in Holmes Terrace had been refurbished and transformed into a central policing base for frontline officers and detectives attached to the London South Area, and this also happened to come under Heather's remit at present. It was set right next to the busy thoroughfare of Waterloo station and had grown over the years to include a number of community support officers, special constables and valued support staff. It was without doubt, one of the busiest stations and it also had a good reputation for achieving excellent results in terms of detecting and deterring crime on both the streets and railways.

As arranged, Liberty pulled up into the disabled bay in the small but busy car park just after ten that morning, once a lorry causing a slight traffic jam had been sorted out. Having then scrambled to get into her wheelchair, due to space limitations and not wanting to be run over by two of the larger vans moving back and forth nearby, she eventually made her way over to the main entrance and thankfully entered the air-conditioned reception area. A female officer, who'd spotted her from where she stood behind the counter, smiled as she entered the building and instantly started to work her way out to her. She'd immediately recognized who she was as they'd known each other for a good many years. Yet despite that fact, she still needed to double check Liberty's identity as per the high-level security procedures that needed following with no exceptions. With the formalities soon over, another officer was called around to escort her and although she'd seen him before, this man just led her to the lift without saying very much for himself.

Once inside, Liberty pressed the button for the fourth floor as instructed. Although she'd never had any real reason to think about it before, or even notice for that reason, she was more than pleased to see the whole thing had been designed with space and a modern specification that fully met the requirements for someone like her in this day and age of so-called awareness. Much to her surprise, Detective Inspector Dave Light greeted her in the corridor as soon as the lift doors had opened and Liberty had wheeled herself out into a bit of space that would allow others to pass. She and Dave had spoken many times, both on the phone, and when they'd met up in person at some of the quarterly meetings they'd been expected to attend in their positions.

He was one of the nicer guys who always remained professional and was always more than willing to help if asked. Dave was slightly younger than her at fifty-two years old. He was classed as being reasonably tall, at six foot four. He had dark hair that was slightly balding in places but still not showing any signs of greying just yet. She had no doubt he was more than likely very handsome when he was in his youth, although she never remembered their paths ever seeming to cross in the early days. His was also a face she most certainly wouldn't have forgotten in a hurry. The man also maintained a good, firm hand grip, which was always a good point in her eyes. She really wasn't a great lover of limp wristed men who she felt a feeble handshake from was a sign of weakness and possible lack of confidence. Having asked if it was okay before doing so, Dave happily wheeled her in between a combination of desks that were very similar to those that stood in her own department. Likewise, they were all filled with monitors and ten-ton of much needed computer equipment set out in the large open plan area that had also been purposely put in place during the refurbishment. Dave didn't have his own office, as everyone was supposed to be working on a level playing field allegedly. He gave her one of those knowing looks as he set about explaining that part to her, once they were finally at his desk and had sorted out some room for her wheelchair. An officer who she judged to be in his early to mid-twenties suddenly approached from behind, and after having been introduced as a support officer who was currently helping out with some of the admin work, Lawrence Daley asked if the pair of them would be needing any drinks at all.

'Coffee would be brilliant for me,' Dave answered, before turning to peer over at Liberty.

'Yeah, same for me thanks,' Liberty added, with a somewhat cheeky grin.

True to his offer, a few minutes later they both sat with a steaming mug of coffee each and started off their conversation.

Liberty gave Dave a full run down on the latest, which was not much more than she'd already told him over the phone earlier. A minute later, Liberty tilted her head over to look down at a couple of photographs that Dave had fished around for in a labelled folder and then placed before her on the desk. The DI then bashed away at his keypad and nodded his head as if praising himself before pulling up some files on his computer. Liberty watched as he continued to click away at a few of the folders marked up on the left-hand side until he finally appeared to find the one he was after.

'Why's it always harder to find what you want in the system when you have someone with you or you're in a hurry? He asked.

'I'm exactly the same in all honesty,' Liberty replied straightaway. 'Sadly, I also have the same problem with all the crap that's stored up inside my head when I need it urgently.'

Although, she didn't get taken out for lunch, because Dave unfortunately got called in about something to do with another case he was working on, Liberty still felt she'd done quite well to get two half decent cups of coffee out of them. Lawrence had obviously been trained well, unless of course, that was only for show when certain guests arrived. The whole meeting had still been well worthwhile however, as Liberty now had a name for the train victim as a Mr David Boston. According to the records, he'd been the Managing Director of a company over in New Malden and it sounded as if he hadn't been there for very long before becoming a victim. The guy was divorced apparently, and therefore Dave had suggested she may be better off going and having a face-to-face chat with the Office Manager named Debbie Drinkwater. She'd been really helpful apparently, yet Dave had also felt she'd been holding back on something that Liberty may just well be able to charm out of her.

*

It was nearing two o'clock in the afternoon when Liberty's black VW Caddy pulled into one of the two disabled parking bays located just outside the small parade of shops. The car sitting in the other bay showed no sign of a blue disability permit being displayed in its window and it looked incredibly flash and sporty. Therefore, Liberty suspected the driver wasn't entitled to be there, which annoyed her in some respects, but wasn't really her job to do something about. Liberty knew she still had a short way to go herself, as she'd still need to cross the road and work her way down a short bendy hill before she came to the place she was after.

Unfortunately, parking any closer was pretty much out of the question as that particular stretch of the road was a well-known black spot where drivers tended to drive far too fast and take the bend as if they were driving on some sort of race track. Reaching over and switching off the ignition on her specially adapted dashboard, Liberty hurriedly turned to Helen, who'd used the journey to add a touch of makeup to her face, and now sat looking over at her from the passenger seat awaiting further instructions.

'Are you sure this information is what we're after?' she asked. 'Some of the stuff we've been getting from your source has been a bit screwed up just lately.'

Liberty smiled as she nodded and started to reach for the wheelchair release. 'I admit he's been a bit crap the last couple of times I've used him, but we really don't have much else to go on at the present time. If you look at it the other way though, he's essentially got to come up with a winner sometime soon, if you work out the odds.'

'If you say so boss.' Helen replied, trying to suppress her laugh as she got out and walked to the back of the vehicle. She stood and watched with interest as the tailgate and ramp did their business and allowed her boss to exit completely unaided with much less noise that anyone would expect. Liberty took a moment to hit the remote again and the boot closed up automatically as both women stared in wonder at how modern technology had advanced so much, even in their short lifetimes.

'You know I'm not a betting woman, yet I'm only saying that because I really don't want us to be wasting any time chasing up false hopes when we have so many other things still sitting on our plate. Liberty wasn't about to admit it, but she also held the same sort of feelings deep down, and she wasn't exactly convinced with her lead.

'I'll tell you what. Let's just give this a try first, and then you can tell me *I told you so* if the whole thing turns out to be a complete and utter waste of time. Right now, I could really do with a spot of fresh air if that makes you feel any better?'

A few minutes later they were going downhill and sticking quite sensibly to the pavement on the right-hand side of the road. Liberty's mobile phone rang about halfway down and she answered immediately.

'That was Heather,' she informed Helen, once she'd

managed to finish her conversation and hang up. According to the latest Intel she's received, she thinks we may well be onto something here. She's saying we need to remain fairly cautious in what we do, as we're purportedly dealing with an unstable youngster who's somewhat anxious about the whole thing. Evidentially, this tied in with something she's heard from one of her friends who just happens to know the woman who's in charge of the place we're going to.'

'Well I guess we'd better get our arses in gear.' Helen replied, as she wheeled her boss ahead of her, just before spotting and having to negotiate a broken pavement that jutted up at from the side of the road.

*

'Good morning, Mike,' came the welcoming greeting. This was closely followed by a rock-solid handshake from the Head of Operations as part of the show. He was a lanky, ginger haired man by the name of Wayne Smith who'd been given the job of hosting the auditor for the day.

'Can I get you a tea or coffee?' He asked, with an energy that nobody should ever really have been allowed to exude so early on in the working day.

'Thanks Wayne, I'd like a tea, white with no sugar if that's okay please,' Mike replied, without even giving his answer a second thought before stifling a yawn. He then covered his mouth as he started to yawn again before setting up his laptop and finding an electric socket to plug his charger into, prior to taking a seat in the meeting room he'd been shown into.

'There was some sort of night-time road works going on outside my place last night, so I didn't get a great deal of sleep.' He initially lied to Wayne, not wishing to explain the fact that his flatmate Jenny had come into his room in the middle of the night acting incredibly horny, which unsurprisingly led to quite a number of wild sessions of unadulterated sex. She'd now done this a total of three times since their first get together on the sofa, and she was more than adamant that Tom really wasn't bothered despite knowing what she was up to. Mike still felt guilty however, and he'd even found it a little bit awkward around Tom at times, despite enjoying himself every time she'd visited him. Mike set about removing a few more things that he needed from his shoulder bag before starting the audit as he and Wayne sat and caught up with everything that had happened since the previous meeting.

 'I assume that's not a regular thing each night?' Wayne asked with a grin, once the real reason for Mike being so tired had finally emerged. Mike laughed inwardly as he wondered if that vixen Jenny really did have such plans. He'd never be able to keep up with her if that ever happened, plus she was probably getting her fill with Tom beforehand, which was something he'd rather not think about. Getting back to reality, once the Managing Director and Quality Manager had both arrived in the boardroom and gone through all the necessary formalities of handshakes and small talk, Mike finally turned his thoughts back to the audit and began the opening meeting.

*

Continuing on down the steep hill and avoiding a few of the dodgier looking paving slabs, they eventually approached what looked like a factory of some kind. This was situated just off the road to the left-hand side with a small car park that contained around half a dozen cars all boxed in by a large delivery van.

As they drew closer to the unit, the whole thing looked quite dilapidated on the outside, yet Liberty knew from years of experience that this would most likely prove to be a big red herring, as it would doubtless be the same on the inside. According to records on the company, The Managing Director - Paul Rowlandson had acquired overall control of the place from his two partners' way back in 1976. Then, and in line with the ever-changing political and economic circumstances over the years that followed, whilst in association with his unwavering commitment to producing quality products, the man then put his money where his mouth was and invested in new technology. This proved well worthwhile as the company gradually built up a strong reputation in the engineering sector and became a talking point in some circles. When Paul eventually chose to retire in 1998, with a heart by-pass also adding to this decision, control remained within the family with his daughter Angela finally taking the reins and becoming MD in 2009.

The place now hosted a full range of CNC milling and grinding machines with a decent range of state-of-the-art inspection equipment that had been added just over two years ago. Angela's justification was that the company now had a base of operations in a modern workshop which housed some of the latest technology and equipment with some of the greatest expertise being maintained internally. This covered a number of industries which ensured customers benefitted from the most cost-effective, quality-assured methods of precision engineering, allegedly. Whether you believed that or not was down to your own personal viewpoint, but getting inside had certainly thrown up its own challenges, which was something that Liberty was gradually getting used to.

Once they were in the meeting room, Angela was very apologetic about Liberty having to be re-routed via the delivery bay in her wheelchair. Evidently, they didn't have any disabled staff working for them right now, but they were looking into what legislation applied to them as a business, especially as the plans to refurbish the outside were still ongoing.

Casting the subject quickly aside, one of Angela's young, male apprentices was welcomed into the room and instantly introduced to Liberty and Helen. Both women could see quite clearly how nervous the youngster appeared to be, but neither of them reacted and decided to see how things would pan out.

'Listen Sean, there's no need to worry about anything at all.' Helen stated, as she happily took the lead, seeing as this had already been pre-arranged beforehand.

'We're only here to gather any information you may happen to be holding about what you witnessed at the shopping mall on the day in question. It could prove very important and allow us to move on quite considerably with the case we're currently working on. Anything you can tell us could prove to be vital information, and in all honesty, we really could do with something fresher to go on right now.

Angela has already been kind enough to explain how you eventually confided in her. Apparently, you've been worrying about the whole event ever since it first happened. We see this quite a lot in our job and it's only natural, so don't feel guilty about the fact you've taken a while to come forward and say anything. The main thing is that you're now feeling ready to talk, and that's a good thing.' At that point, Helen then leaned over and pulled something from her bag before opening up the file she'd retrieved as this was something she'd already prepared for the meeting. A moment later she placed a printed photo from the CCTV footage face up on the table.

'This is what we have at the moment. It's not a great deal as you can see. However, anything that springs to mind or chooses to jog your memory right now will be more than gratefully accepted, I assure you.' There was an odd moment of silence in the room while Sean gazed down at the image and recollected what had happened. All three onlookers awaited some sort of reaction. From the instant it had happened and right up until now, this was what Sean had been trying to shake off. The very image of the businessman dropping like a stone over the barrier holding his neck and acting as if he'd been stung, almost instantly came flying back to him with all guns blazing.

'The one wearing the hoodie did it.' he muttered, before tears suddenly filled his eyes and the youngster broke down and became an emotional wreck.

*

Liberty was informed about a report that hadn't long come through about a man allegedly threatening staff with a needle at Surbiton railway station. Local officers were said to have arrived at the scene within a matter of minutes where a chase through the busy high street had ensued before he'd finally been caught and arrested. There was no particular reason to suspect he may have been the same killer they were after, as the officer's reports showed him as being a known person who suffered with mental health problems. As the guy was being brought into their station anyway, combined with the fact that she had nothing to lose by seeing him anyway, Liberty was more than happy to go downstairs to interview him, even if it was just to eliminate him from their investigation. There weren't any details on the type of needle he'd been threatening people with, so in all reality it could have been a knitting needle or nothing like that at all. She'd just have to wait and see, because nine times out of ten, things were never quite what you'd expect them to be.

Forty-five minutes later, sat with 46-year-old, Billy Chandler sitting across from her in one of the interrogation rooms, Liberty was not willing to give way to all the crap the man was spewing out about this, that and the other. She knew Billy was trying his best to provoke her into losing her cool, but Liberty had become a hardened professional over the years. Therefore, she simply bit her top lip in order to steady herself and to bring her way of thinking back to the place it should've been, before being slightly side-tracked. The DCI was aware that her head was burning with a blend of both anger and frustration, so she took a long deep breath to help her gain the strength she so needed to carry on. Gazing over, Liberty could see that Billy's cold, icy stare had settled upon her once again and noted it also seemed very detached in a strange kind of way. That gave her no doubt whatsoever that he was on some form of medication, although she also suspected there were most likely a few other substances that had been added through less salubrious means. The guy most definitely had issues and wasn't quite right in the head, but Liberty needed answers and refused to be intimidated by the man sitting before her. She'd known it was always going to be a battle right from the moment she'd spoken with the arresting officers and then stepped inside the room. Yet true to form; she'd simply carried on with her line of questioning as if he were any other suspect she'd ever questioned, despite knowing one hundred percent that he wasn't the person they were after. Almost laughably, it had turned out that the so-called 'needle' had in fact been a small umbrella, and this just served to demonstrate how many of the initial reports that came in could often prove to be so very wide of the mark. Finishing up the interview and treating it as a favour that could hopefully be returned at some time in the future, Billy Chandler was thankfully led away to be held elsewhere while the necessary paperwork was sorted out and the right people could be notified so someone from outside could come along to the station and collect him.

'Well that was a complete waste of time.' Liberty thought, as she wheeled herself out to the lift.

*

Luke King had only joined the police because it had been the sort of job he'd always wanted to do as a young boy and then taken the first opportunity after seeing an advert in the local paper. Nothing else had ever gone right for him since leaving school four-years ago, or at least that was the way it seemed through his eyes. Luke was a fairly tall guy, a bit baby-faced and incredibly clumsy at times, although he did prefer to keep himself to himself, whenever and wherever possible. His confidence had certainly been dented on more than one occasion. He'd proved useless as a salesman, even more so as a shop assistant and had even served a stint as a postman, which only lasted three weeks after he'd managed to allow a whole batch of letters to get totally ruined in the rain. He was generally seen as a nice enough chap, reasonably intelligent and someone with a decent sense of humour, according to a few people at least. Yet Luke had always known deep down inside that there was something more. He'd just have to find something a little more challenging, which may well have had a lot to do with his past failures, according to his line of rational.

Having been through many of the tougher parts of the job and finally managing to get to work with the likes of the infamous DCI Liberty Rock and her team, Luke King felt he'd be more than likely to be able to settle down at long last. Fortunately for him, even Cheryl Burgess as the other newbie who'd only just joined the team had also proved to be very nice and thoughtful, plus she'd even been kind enough to help him out on a few of the more awkward occasions where he maybe hadn't quite grasped something he should have. It wasn't that he was slow or anything like that; it was simply his lack of self-belief and the fact that his pride always had a strange need to come first. He knew they were having a tough time trying to get him to open up every now and again, and he also realised he was his own worst enemy at times. He really needed to be more trusting in other people, but at least he was aware and working on it. Luke fully recognized it was only a matter of time before everything finally clicked into place, or at least he hoped so.

'Who knows!' he thought. 'If the job worked out fine,

then he may even gain enough confidence to ask out the pretty looking woman who appeared to live alone in the flat next door to where he was living at the moment.' She was always smiling at him and almost seemed begging for him to strike up some sort of conversation. Soon, it had to be soon. Luke had been certain this job would finally be the making of him once he managed to get his head around everything. Once that happened, they'd all see an entirely different character begin to emerge. He'd be a shining example and one of the team. Someone they'd all be more than happy to rely on. He just needed to keep telling himself that and stop filling his head with negative thoughts.

CHAPTER 6

Having pulled up in the front forecourt of the business they'd been on the lookout for over in New Malden, this lay in a road just a little way off from the main high street. Liberty parked her monstrous sized car in a disabled parking bay, whose paintwork provided very faint road markings, and was in desperate need of a decent, long-overdue makeover. Helen stepped out into the biting wind and gazed up at the four-storey office building. That was when she noticed a woman, with what she viewed to be long blonde hair gazing down at them from one of the first-floor windows. She'd been giving them both what she classed as being a half-hearted wave before eventually turning away and moving out of view.

Stepping down from the passenger side of the Caddy and walking around to the back of the vehicle, Helen was already used to finding Liberty in complete control with the wheelchair already shooting down the ramp. She'd already grown oblivious to the protests whenever she tried to offer assistance once she was down, and in all honesty, Liberty wasn't really all that bothered when it involved her wonderful partner. She still liked to make her think she was angry, although Helen was probably the only human being alive who she'd allow to push her along the road. God forbid anyone else who tried to lend a hand. Liberty really wasn't up for anything like that just yet, although Heather would probably be the other only exception to the rule.

Passing over a section of the car park loaded with bumpy gravel that was impossible to avoid and with Liberty being shaken all over the place as they did so, Helen eventually managed to guide the wheelchair onto the smoother part of a path and then on through a small wooden gate that separated the car park from the main building. Shutting it closed behind them with a horrible squeaky sound coming from its rusty hinges in their wake, they quickly followed the sign to the reception where Helen reached over and pressed a small metal push button that was needed to open the larger side door. They'd never have been stupid enough to tackle the hefty glass revolving door that stood beside it. That was something they'd learnt from a previous experience and they certainly weren't about to fall for it again.

Following a short wait just inside and having already announced who they were and who they wished to see to the receptionist, the lift suddenly broadcast its arrival with a loud audible ding. As the doors opened, Helen recognised the blonde woman as the one who'd been watching them arrive from the upstairs window. It was easy to spot she hadn't been sleeping too well as of late, as the woman appeared rather drawn and weary looking with both detectives sympathising completely when it came to being so damned tired.

'It's good to meet the both of you,' Debbie stated, offering her hand and then shaking both of theirs in turn. She then turned to the reception desk and pointed out the visitor's book before asking the pair of them to sign in with Helen going first then handing it down to Liberty so that she could do the honours. Debbie then handed them both visitors' badges which also held fobs on the lanyards that she confirmed would allow them to get around the building unaided.

'We had the building refurbished four-years ago to allow for disabled access,' she informed Liberty directly, then went a little red as the DCI stared straight back at her. 'The car park does need a touch of paint I'm afraid, and I'm sorry about the gravel,' she added, assuming that was the reason she'd been given such an intense stare. Helen certainly hadn't missed the exchange and quickly made amends by giving the woman a nice friendly smile as they entered the lift, before informing her that Liberty was still trying to come to terms with certain things that being disabled seemed to throw up at her every day.

'Don't take it personally,' she assured her as they moved into the corridor and followed her to one of the meeting rooms where they could chat undisturbed. Liberty knew what was being said but took no notice as other; more important things were busy working away inside her head.

'Please take a seat and make yourselves comfortable,' she told them. 'I'll take this opportunity to say sorry in advance if it's a bit cold in here at the moment. The landlords been having a bit of work done on the boiler system, so the engineers have had to drain it all down. Unfortunately, that in turn, has managed to leave the building without any heating for now. It sounds like there's always something being done to the building I guess,' she added, all apologetically, before carrying on.

'There are no planned fire drills today and I'd ask you to please follow me out of the building in the event of a fire. We're only on the first floor, so getting the wheelchair down the stairs shouldn't take too long I hope, so where do you wish to start first? She quickly asked, changing the subject and taking a seat opposite them with both Liberty and Helen having already turned down the offer of tea or coffee on the way in.

Debbie Drinkwater had been born and raised in Lowestoft, Suffolk. She therefore carried a slight accent that was noticed much more distinctively in certain words that she used. Debbie was short at five foot two and although she wasn't what certain people would class the most beautiful of women; there was still something quite attractive about her. It had already been noted that she also had one of the most wonderful smiles, one that could easily light up a room with very little or no effort whatsoever. Debbie had worked at the company for the last twelve years as the Office Manager and been deemed pretty much part of the furniture until Gerry Barnes had finally decided to bid them all farewell and retire from his role as the head of the company. When David Boston had arrived and taken his place, everything had pretty much changed almost overnight. Some members of staff had got up and left soon after, but many had eventually been laid off with David having used a whole number of sneaky ways to ensure that they'd left with nothing, which gave little doubt that he'd used these tactics many times before.

The two detectives came away from the meeting with not

much more than knowing the guy was a nasty piece of work who would have formed many enemies during his working life. It was never nice to hear about people dying, and although their remit was to try to reduce this from happening, there were still people that even they felt sometimes got their just rewards. Although they were both aware that feeling like that was wrong, they were still both human at the end of the day, despite what some people thought about those who worked for the police force.

*

Liberty received the call on her mobile around ten-to-two in the afternoon, just as she and Helen had been about to head back to her car after having stopped to grab some lunch.

'What's up Cheryl?' she asked the newbie, holding the phone close to her ear. 'Alright, that's good. Thanks for letting us know so quickly, we'll head straight there.' Ending the call, Liberty shouted up at Helen, who'd continued to wheel her along while the call had been in progress. 'It looks as if we have another one on our plate Hel's. This one's female though.'

By the time they got to the car park that ran alongside the large glass office building with its towering shadow encompassing the space below and making it feel quite cold, a crowd had already gathered. Three police cars and an ambulance were present with a couple of the police working to ensure the onlookers didn't get out of hand or stray any further. They stood telling them there was nothing to see and to go back to work. The detectives had already been recognised and had no need to show their ID. The officer who they'd guessed was in charge, soon walked across to them as soon as he'd finished his conversation with another colleague.

 Then, after a short discussion; he promptly escorted them to the rear end of the car park where the body had been found. Staring down at the dead woman, the paramedics confirmed she'd already been dead when they'd arrived at the scene. They'd made sure not to disturb anything and confirmed that the security guard, who'd stumbled across the body during his patrol, was now inside the building trying to recover from the shock.

*

The following morning was just as dull as the previous one with the sky very overcast and a sudden downpour occurring as soon as Helen stepped out into the street. The bitter wind blowing across her as she headed towards her car felt no better, and by the time she'd reached her destination and sat behind the wheel, she was cold, wet and pretty pissed off. The case didn't seem to be moving as fast as she and Liberty had hoped, so there was an update due to take place as soon as she reached work. Listening to 5 Live on the radio, she laughed as the weather forecast mentioned it was raining heavily in her area. Scratching her nose as she drove and being careful not to catch herself with her fingernails, Helen was annoyed that she'd had a bad night following an argument with Mark. He was really starting to annoy her by feeling sorry for himself all the time and being such a miserable git. Sure, they'd all been through hard times during the case with the two serial killers who'd worked together along with all the SERIS team crap that had happened. She also had a good idea of what he'd suffered with the torture and having been left for dead, yet that didn't justify why he'd changed and become such a burden to live with. Liberty and numerous others had all had some sort of shit happen to them at one time or another, but they'd all managed to just get on with their lives and not bring it up every two seconds like Mark seemed to be doing. Helen wasn't sure how much more she could take right now. It certainly wasn't looking too good, and she sure as hell wasn't going to put up with that nonsense much longer. She was still an independent woman and certainly had no qualms about going solo again.

*

'As with all the victims phone records, we've had checks carried out with base stations identified, held interviews in shops, bars and anywhere else we could have got a lead from, but nothing's come up at all. We've checked social media sites and talked to friends and relatives but drawn a blank each time, so we're still getting nowhere fast.'

Liberty continued on and covered details most of the team were already aware of. Lorraine Carey had been found murdered early that morning in the car park with the cause of death still to be confirmed. If her theory was right, it looked to be as a result of being injected with a strong dose of succinylcholine in the neck, which would have totally disabled her body and led to eventual heart failure. There'd been no witnesses, or none that had come forward so far, although investigations were still continuing and they still awaited results from the lab. Liberty didn't hold much hope however. The killer had been very clever up until now, and forensics hadn't turned up anything so far. She could quite clearly see for herself that most of the team were feeling pretty pissed off. A few even sat with their arms completely crossed, plus she'd already noticed a few yawns happen to occur during her speech. They all knew the ups and downs that came with the job, but they were a good team and she knew they'd fully nail it in the end. Now would possibly be a good time to give them one of her rousing motivational speeches to get them all up and running again.

'We all came into this job wanting to make a change in some way. We wanted to make the streets safer so that our friends and family had a decent environment in which we could all live, work and feel comfortable in. That's why we do what we do, and that's why we have to raise our game and work together as a team, even when we feel we're getting nowhere fast. We don't give up, and we certainly won't let those criminals out there think they have the freedom to come and go and do whatever they please.'

Liberty gained a short handclap for that and hoped she hadn't come across as too American like the crap often seen on some of those TV crime shows. She knew the sceptics amongst them, but valued them all. She was however, a little worried about Helen. She looked tired yet knew that was partly down to what was going on between her and Mark at the moment. The other one that worried her was the newbie, Luke King. He seemed to be struggling a little, but his pride seemed to come first, and they were having a tough time trying to get him to open up.

It wouldn't have been very fair to ask Cheryl to work on him, as that could complicate matters and look as if they were favouring her over him.

Liberty glanced down at her watch and registered that the meeting had taken just under forty-five minutes, which was pretty good going. One of the team stood holding the door open for her, so she politely thanked him and then wheeled her way back to her desk with Helen having already disappeared to get them both a hot drink.

*

Liberty sat at her desk with her wheelchair facing outwards. Helen stood next to her with her feet planted firmly on the floor and her hands behind her head looking just as frustrated as they both tried to gather their thoughts.

'We just need a decent lead right now. I know we're on the right track but something's not right and I just can't seem to put my finger on it.' Helen gazed down at her boss and knew she'd just told her exactly how she felt right now. It could be a very testing part of the job when it happened, but the trick was to battle on and stick with your gut instinct.

'Let's just run over everything we have so far and check if we've missed anything. It's probably something simple that's staring us right in the face, but we're both delving far too deep and missing it somehow.' Helen added, in an attempt to lift their spirits and get them back on track. She was due to visit the morgue later, so at least they'd have more answers after that.

*

Tim Mears, the Pathologist, pointed at the screen as all eyes focused firmly on the image.

'You can see the mark quite clearly around the area where the needle punctured Lorraine Carey's neck

71

while she was in the car park.....'

Helen stood watching but felt incredibly tired, having suffered yet another frustrating evening with Mark. She tried hard to ignore the weariness but it wasn't all that easy, especially in such cold surroundings. Having got to know the place and learnt about the people who did such a job for a living, Helen had already realised it was the morticians who were the real workers in the morgue. It was them that carried out the hard labour in the shadow of the pathologist, although they'd often come across as a fairly weird bunch, being cliquey and secretive at times. On the plus side, they all seemed to be very down to earth and knowledgeable on all sorts of crazy topics once you gained their respect.

Helen and Tim went into much further detail as they worked through the evidence together via a selection of photographs, detailed measurements and other elements gathered from the crime scene by the forensics team, that could prove so crucial to the investigation at a later date. Tim was on his best behaviour for a change, as he and Helen shared a few thoughts based around information they'd already compiled from the previous murders. It was like trying to put one of those really complex puzzles together which always took longer than expected to form a picture and see the whole story. It felt as if the killer was playing with them and had the upper hand. That only added to the pressure making it all the more important to bring the case to a close before any further murders took place. Helen knew from experience there'd be a painful waiting period before the full facts to bring a killer to justice in court finally emerged. Much of this depended on the autopsies having been completed with the i's dotted and the t's crossed as per the strict protocol's dictated within the legal system. On any occasion where a death occurred under suspicious circumstances, or where no signs of natural causes could be found, an autopsy would be required to take place. Just to add to the red tape and delay things even further, detectives investigating the case had to notify the coroner's office of their need before copies of reports would finally be sent to them. All of this had to be done via the correct channels or you'd get diddly-squat back and get nowhere fast.

The visit hadn't gone quite as Helen expected, having discussed what may happen earlier with Liberty, as she was tied up with another meeting, despite doing her best to get out of it. Tim hadn't been himself, and seemed out of salts, with none of the cheeky smiles or winks that he usually gave. Even the offer of lunch failed to materialise, so maybe the pressure of work was finally starting to get to him as well. They had looked incredibly busy, Helen confirmed, as she removed her protective overalls and latex gloves before placing them in the biohazard bin prior to washing her hands with antimicrobial soap from the dispenser just above the wash basin. She hadn't handled anything and hadn't planned too, especially as the image of Tim messing with a brain was still firmly etched in her memory from an earlier visit.

That certainly hadn't been one of her better moments in the job, and as she put her jacket back on and waved farewell to Tim through the glass, she seriously hoped Liberty was having a better time at her meeting.

CHAPTER 7

Mark had been sitting on the sofa with his eyes glued to the TV screen watching one of those crap quiz shows he always complained about once Helen returned home.

The nights were drawing in and it had started to get a lot colder over the last few days, so Helen was thankful she'd bothered to set the heating to come on an hour earlier. She was the technical one in the house, as Mark didn't even have a clue on how to adjust the TV. The remote control was confusing for him, unless of course, it involved the simple action of turning it on and selecting a channel. On demand, and any other features also proved just as impossible for him to negotiate. That would get him into a right strop at times, but Helen didn't doubt for one moment that that was any different from most homes across the country.

With her favourite coffee cup all patterned with bright red roses for herself, and a tea without sugar for Mark, Helen entered the living room being careful not to spill anything before setting them down on the wooden tables then sitting beside her man on the sofa.

'So, what's the latest?' He asked half-heartedly, still staring at the screen.

'This case with the killer using some kind of needle to kill people really needs to be sorted out sooner rather than later as there's a load of pressure coming down from above for some reason. That stuff in the press along with speculation out there on social media sites doesn't exactly help matters,' she added. 'Liberty doesn't know I'm aware, but you know what the grapevine in that place is like. Your lot are no different either, are they?'

'No, I guess not.' Mark muttered, still only half paying attention as Helen ranted on about this, that and the other before finally getting up to make something to eat for the evening. She was incredibly restless and really needed to do something to take her mind off things for a while. They were honestly turning into an old, married couple already, and Helen was really starting to hate coming home just lately. It wasn't a good place to be from a mindset perspective right now, with the main problem being she still felt very guilty about what had happened to Mark. This just made the whole thing fester even more as time went on, and it certainly wasn't the healthiest of lifestyles for either of them. What was the answer though? It was probably staring her right in the face, but damned if she could put her finger on it.

*

Liberty was sitting on the sofa knitting. She was thinking about Helen and how she'd gotten on with Tim down at the morgue, while she'd been stuck at some boring meeting about the latest changes to regulations that would supposedly have some sort of impact on the work they did in the future.

Helen was spirited and beautiful. She always backed her up whenever she needed someone to be there or watch over her, and was one of the most genuinely, caring people she'd ever met.

Right now, she seemed to be going through a whole load of shit with Mark, yet Liberty felt totally useless as the woman wouldn't allow her to help in any way. Liberty knew something was up because she could read her partner like a book, and the misery showing on her face just lately was not that of the person she usually worked with. Liberty felt seriously worried and let out a huge sigh before dropping a stitch and cursing out loud. In all respect to Helen, the woman wasn't allowing it to interfere with her work, or at least Liberty hadn't noticed anything untoward so far. But she still needed her partner to be ready to roll if needed. Just then, she dropped another stitch followed by one of her knitting needles slipping down the side of the sofa before the swearing started again. What on earth had possessed her to take up the stupid thing in the first place? Liberty began to laugh as she remembered the whole idea was to calm her down and make sure she did something for herself for a change.

'Some chance.' She blurted out to no one but herself. 'Now, where's that bloody needle gone?'

*

As she was driving to work the next day, Liberty remembered reading about cases similar to some of hers as well as catching live broadcasts and TV programmes that covered past investigations. There was obviously a hunger from the public for this sort of thing, because so many shows like CSI and the like were proving very successful when it came down to ratings. These shows drilled down into historic murders, recreated the original crime scenes and then set about solving cases with the latest techniques and gadgetry. Nothing was sacred any longer. Everything was on show and it was no wonder the criminals were getting wiser, which certainly didn't make her job any easier.

*

Later in the afternoon, Liberty and Helen took the road that headed towards the local industrial estate with its unavoidable sign marked 'The Thamesdale'. They entered the main service road a short while later, having noted there was no indication of any estate security, which left anyone able to enter the place unchallenged. A few sections of the perimeter wall had rusty barbed wire on display and the gate was shut at night, yet that still didn't stop the local hooligans from getting in if they wanted to.

 Pulling up outside the unit they were seeking and studying it from inside the car, this one appeared to be slightly different from the neighbouring ones. Although it seemed deserted for now, something didn't look right and both women felt they were being watched. They'd gained a tip off about the building a few days earlier and just needed to get an idea of what it was like. Rumour had it that something big was going to go down fairly soon.
 'Interesting place', Helen uttered, with a very tongue in cheek expression underlying what she meant.

Just at that moment, one of the side doors opened and a young man appeared before heading across, jangling his keys towards one of the vehicles parked just behind them. With no point hiding the fact that they'd been seen, Liberty pressed the button to lower the window and then called out to him. They watched as the figure stopped dead still in his tracks, but still gave the impression that he'd wanted to get away in a bit of a hurry.

He was tall and gangly looking, and as he drew closer, with a brief moment of hesitation they noticed he had quite a spotty face with puffy cheeks that looked a bit odd in comparison with the rest of his frame. Not knowing they were from the police, he automatically started to act all cocky once he realised they were alone, although he did let out a slightly strange look when he caught sight of the wheelchair.

'I'd bugger off if I were you,' he advised. 'There's no one around and it's starting to get dark. It's not exactly the best of areas to be caught in ladies.'

It sounded a bit condescending, but Liberty understood his concern before asking if he'd heard of another company she knew were based on the same estate. Confirming he'd been in a hurry, the man gave directions and then shot off as quickly as he could, although he still showed off with a wheel spin.

Having already made her decision, Liberty started the car and drove off prior to doing a circuit of the block and returning back not long after. This time, she parked slightly further away but made sure they still had a decent view of the front of the building. She wasn't easily put off at the best of times and something inside her really irked her. Both women knew this was never a good sign as they sat watching.

*

Malik really felt he'd landed on his feet when he'd arrived in the UK from Egypt four years previously and been able to put what he termed as *his crappy past* behind him. He was twenty years old and managed to secure a room in the large rented house in Chessington, Surrey. That had been more by luck than judgement, having jumped on a train from Waterloo despite being unsure of where he was heading. The rent had worked out pretty well as it was split between himself and the three housemates he was shacked up with, although he was never quite sure how much Jenny contributed. She spent most nights in Tom's room, despite having her own room right next to his. Still, as long as the rent was paid fully and on time, who cared? It wasn't a massive room he lived in. It was basically a loft extension that had been added on about ten years previously by the owner, who was retired and living out in Spain, according to the others. Yet, the room suited him just fine and had the added bonus of having access to a small roof terrace. He used that in the nicer weather, although it wasn't quite as safe as it should have been, due to the dodgy barrier that was supposed to act as a guardrail, allegedly. Malik was a self-employed IT freak who much preferred his own space and tended to be a bit weird at times, according to his flatmates, who often referred to him as 'the nerd that lived in the attic'. Malik didn't mind the nickname one bit, but they all knew he could prove very sociable when he wanted to be. There were times when he really enjoyed their company, especially Mike, as he always had interesting stories to tell about the work he did with so many different types of characters. He always described them so well that you almost felt you knew them in person before he'd finished speaking.

Tom was much quieter and more macho, or so he believed, yet Jenny was more of an anomaly and someone he couldn't quite figure out. She loved to tease both him and Mike sexually when Tom wasn't around, and she was highly intelligent, although she appeared to cover that up for some strange reason. It also helped that she was quite a looker and scrubbed up well, whenever she chose to, which sadly wasn't that often.

*

Cheryl Burgess knew he was the one she needed to speak to. The man suited the description Liberty had given him perfectly. He approached on the same side of the road and walked with a stride that suggested something wasn't quite right. Once you'd learnt to study people and been given training to provide the tell-tale signs of the different types you'd meet out on the streets, it was something that stayed with you for the rest of your life. On closer inspection, as the man continued to draw closer, Cheryl sensed he had troubles. His eyes were all swollen and puffy looking, plus his flesh was dull and sickly. Her first guess was that he hadn't slept for a while. But once she'd taken a proper look and thought about it a bit further, she realised it was either drink or drugs. He was just passing her by and giving her a cursory glance, but Cheryl spoke his name which caused him to stop dead in his tracks. They stood out in an open area that was quite busy with footfall, so Cheryl felt quite safe as she introduced herself and watched the man's brain slowly take it all in.

Without wasting any further time and getting straight to the point, she asked him to follow up on something Liberty had last spoken about. Despite the fact she had to reiterate what she'd asked him; it wasn't long before he was off and chatting as if he'd known her for years. He only faltered when she'd taken a gamble and tried to step it up a few notches. The man whined a little at first and tried to act as if she was out of order, but the new face on the block just scribbled the details down in her notebook.

'I'm playing this by the book, but it's not a game Baxter. I can play tough if you want me to go down that route, yet I'd rather not. Stop making me repeat everything I've asked you as we'll get nowhere fast and I really can't be bothered. Carry on the way you're going and I'll just walk away, then you'll get nothing, I promise you.' Cheryl was hoping he wouldn't call her bluff and hoped he'd carry on talking.

'Bax, everyone calls me Bax.' He insisted, with a faraway look in his eyes that only confirmed he was high on drugs. The sound of a siren in the distance seemed to disturb him and the man screwed his face up as if he was re-experiencing painful memories from somewhere in his past. Unfortunately, this caused the conversation to end abruptly as Bax turned and disappeared into a dimly lit passageway that ran up the side of one of the larger shops. Deciding there'd been no point in following him, Cheryl glanced down at her notes and felt satisfied that she'd gained something to go on for now. The name Malik had stood out the moment Bax had mentioned it, and that was all she needed for now.

*

Finishing work and having promised to do this on more than one occasion without ever doing so, they'd parked up in the closest disabled parking space available. The weather wasn't exactly at its best, and the wind and rain hampered them as they headed past the shops on the high street. Moments later, Helen opened the door to the wonderfully warm and welcome smell of pizza's cooking in the ovens with fresh dough, cheese and salads being prepared by the chefs behind the counter. Helen asked for a table for two, and then followed the young waitress who gazed all sympathetic at Liberty before showing them to a table and removing one of the chairs to allow her to manoeuvre herself into position. Liberty was already used to such receptions, so she simply bit her tongue and allowed for the youngster's inexperience. She was pretty fed up with getting into stupid spats with people who felt they needed to treat her differently from everyone else, plus it always left her feeling as if she was the bad guy.

The waitress smiled as she returned and handed them a menu each. She pointed out the board on the wall with that day's specials on it before announcing she'd be back, then shot off to help out a family of four who'd just come in and stood waiting to be served, just as the sign inside the door had instructed.

The layout was much of a muchness with most pizza chains franchised across the globe. The place wasn't too busy just yet, and it consisted of four separate areas for diners with its walls covered in large prints of Italy in a mix of grey and reddish-brown's to give them a dated, almost sepia look that tended to be associated with old monochrome photographs from both the nineteenth and early twentieth centuries. It was certainly nice and relaxing, which was just what they needed as the waitress returned after giving them time to settle in before asking what they'd like to drink, and if they were now ready to order.

CHAPTER 8

Waking up alone was something Liberty had become well used to over the years. Some would say she lived a bit of a melancholy existence at times, but she felt she dealt with everything quite well. One of the benefits was not having all the distractions that came with the presence of other people in your home first thing in the morning. This also allowed her mind to shift straight to work mode and focus in on the latest case she was working on. There was a certain sense of freedom that many people wouldn't really be able to appreciate as well as she did. Being in hospital had been similar in some respects, and once she'd gone through the usual rigmarole of showering in her wet room and getting dressed, she sat at the table in her wheelchair and gazed through the newspaper that she'd only managed to half read the day before. Scanning through the pages, one of the stories that caught her eye was about a body discovered in some woods up in the midlands.

'Police have launched a murder inquiry after the body of a man was found in woodlands with a series of multiple injuries and are appealing to members of the public for help to find out who he is.

The man is believed to be aged somewhere between 20 to 30 and was found by a dog walker in an area of land just off Four Mile Lane, in Derby on Wednesday evening at around seven-thirty. He is described as being white, of medium build with long black hair and wearing black clothing with a leather biker jacket. The area has been cordoned off since the discovery and will remain so as the murder investigation continues.

Detective Chief Inspector Gary Hills of the Midlands Major Incident Team, said: 'This is a tragic circumstance where a young man has lost his life and every effort will be made by the force to identify him and find his family. At this early stage of the investigation we have yet to establish his identity and need the public's help to find out who he is. We are fully aware that this will cause concern in the local community but I can assure you that we have a significant team of detectives working on this investigation who will be conducting house-to-house visits as well as carrying out extensive CCTV enquires. We are appealing for anyone with information to come and speak to the police as soon as possible. If you were in the Four Mile Lane area over the last few days and saw anything suspicious, then please get in touch.'

This then gave the contact numbers and incident number, but the whole thing was far too similar to what had happened years previously to Helen's Mark, who'd managed to pull through, although poor Emma Still hadn't been quite as fortunate on that occasion. Liberty tried to recall if she'd ever crossed paths with DCI Gary Hills but nothing came to mind, even though the name sounded a little familiar. Maybe she'd give him a ring. Yet even as she was thinking that, she knew it probably wouldn't happen. Sometimes other forces just preferred to be left to their own devices.

*

Once she'd gained everyone's attention, Helen removed a handful of photos from the file and passed copies around for the team to study. The subject looked foreign and in his mid-twenties at a guess. He was quite a handsome looking young man with black curly hair, a slightly crooked looking nose that may have been the result of an accident of some kind, with a square jaw that enhanced his looks and gave him a certain movie star appearance. Liberty sat at the front of the room ready to provide any support if needed, but knew her partner was more than capable of doing an excellent job. Once you'd carried out a few of these briefings, it tended to get easier unless there was a particularly difficult case, especially where the death of a young child or person's known to a member of the team was involved.

'This is Malik Amari,' she continued. 'He's twenty-four, a complete IT geek, self-employed with his own business designing websites, and it just so happens that he lives in the loft extension of a large rented house in Chessington where our auditor friend Mike Britton lives with two other flatmates. Their names are Tom Jones; not the singer I'm sorry to say for all those fans out there, and Jenny Manson who also happens to be Tom's girlfriend.' Everyone sat in silence as they waited to hear what the young man's story was going to be.

'As you already know, Mike Britton was ruled out of the killings as we've now established that he was elsewhere when the murders happened. You've all worked very hard to substantiate each of those events, for which you deserve thanks for a job well done. Having begun looking into the background of Mike's flatmates and seeing as we didn't have all that much to go on at the time, Mr Amari's past just happened to show up as being very interesting indeed. Cheryl has also confirmed this with some interesting Intel she managed to gain out on the street just recently.

Malik Amari was born and bred in Egypt but came to the UK to live four years ago under what appears to be a bit of a cloud. Apparently, when he was back at home, he had a girlfriend who'd been sleeping around with his best mate behind his back for quite a while. It appears that the two of them happened to die in a mysterious house fire not long before Malik arrived over here, but although the police out there were never fully able to prove anything as such, that still doesn't mean the guy's as sweet and innocent as he looks in that picture.

Moving forward, interviews with his friends and family seem to indicate that he'd changed and become quite reclusive just before he decided to leave the country, much to the astonishment of his parents. So, let's just see what else we can find and then we'll set up a surveillance team once we get the go ahead to do so'.

Helen went on to provide further updates on other things that were outstanding before answering a couple of questions, one of which Liberty had to help out with before finally being able to bring the meeting to a close.

*

'So, do we have any more information on that

manager from that dodgy antiques company?' Liberty asked, as she wheeled herself over to Cheryl's desk then peered at her screen to see what she was working on. It was only eight-twenty and most of the team were already in and busily working away on their computers without doing it just to make an impression. It was simply part of their remit with each of them well aware that while the killers were out on the loose, innocent people would be prone to die.

Once Cheryl gave confirmation, Liberty pressed her and wanted to know how his alibi had fitted in with what they wanted to know.

'Looks like a bit of a dead-end that one. His partner backed up what he'd said, although there was a short period of time where he'd gone off to fetch them both a Chinese takeaway from one of the local shops.'

'So, are you saying that he's still on our list of suspects or are we ruling him out altogether? What's your gut feeling on this one?' She asked. 'I really trust your instincts based on what I've been seeing recently, and you my dear are certainly going places if you carry on like that.' Cheryl really didn't know what to say for once, and with her boss sitting so close, she hoped her facial expression wasn't too much of a giveaway that she was more than pleased at what had just been said. They all knew Liberty didn't give away compliments lightly, so Cheryl knew she should make the most of it and savour the moment while it lasted. She also had an appraisal coming up soon, and therefore she needed to continue as she was doing and not screw up between now and then.

'What about information on that warehouse we've been keeping an eye on?' Liberty added.

'That's going to hot up pretty soon. I can feel that one in my bones.'

'I'll chase that one up boss, and see if we've had any further news. They know to contact us if anything changes, but I'll just give them a gentle reminder anyway.'

*

The killer sat catching up with the news on the computer screen and wasn't at all surprised they'd left out the fact that a needle had been used again on that nasty piece of work, Lorraine Carey who seemed to think she ruled the roost at work. Well that was no longer the situation any longer. There was a certain justification that the picture used in the paper wasn't very flattering, plus she didn't come across as being that well liked in the article. Usually everyone said how nice the person was and how they'd be missed so much, but that certainly wasn't the case in this instance, which made the killing even more worthwhile. The figure gave a chuckle as it stood up and walked across to the wardrobe at the other side of the room. Looking at the reflection in the mirror on the inside of the door once opened, the killer smiled and then started to sort through what to wear for the next killing. This was already planned for another business dickhead called Daniel Rosser who worked as a Director in a company that were having an awards event that evening. They'd already viewed the place on Google maps and had a good look around.

The company was called Morotech Limited and fortunately it was only half an hour away. The plan was to dress in a way that would allow them to blend in with the catering staff and get there early enough to have a good look around if possible. Rosser's face was already placed in the memory banks from the profile photograph copied from his Linked in page. The site had security staff and CCTV, but that would be easier to deal with as there'd be a whole multitude of people in the building with lots of food and drink floating around and some form of entertainment going on at some time. There'd be a whole range of distractions, so it was really down to blending in, keeping a close eye on the movements of the victim and striking as soon as the opportunity presented itself. It was getting dark outside and the killer was dressed and ready to go with everything needed to ensure a certain Financial Director never saw the light of the following day, if everything went according to plan.

*

As the surveillance team hadn't come up with anything on Malik Amari just yet, Liberty made the decision to allow Cheryl to conduct the interview with him. She was the one that seemed convinced he was involved in the killings, plus it would be good experience to provide her with a chance to see how Cheryl worked under such circumstances. Liberty had planned to sit and watch the whole thing from behind the one-way mirror, and that's exactly where she sat right now.

Liberty could already sense Malik's nervousness as he sat facing Cheryl on the opposite side of the table and waited for her to begin. As Cheryl studied him further, she switched on the tape recorder, having already run through the full checklist that needed to be communicated before the interview could begin. 'So my first question for you is: Whereabouts were you, either on or around, Thursday the twenty-second of June at twenty-hundred hours?' Malik looked a little puzzled at first, as Liberty stared through the glass and saw him really thinking hard about it. It was always difficult to recollect things when you were put on the spot like that, and she knew Cheryl would have to give him a bit of breathing space in order to come up with an answer sooner or later.

As the interview went on, Liberty jotted down some notes on areas she felt Cheryl could improve on. She'd done quite well so far, and the whole thing was just about to draw to an end, although Malik had grown tired of the entire process and was clearly becoming impatient.

'Can I just ask what time you left the place?' Cheryl asked as she made a few extra notes on her iPad.

'Listen! I've answered these questions already. So, what's the point of repeating things over and over again,' he barked, in annoyance. Cheryl felt he was being very defensive for no real reason and therefore his name was still firmly embedded at the top of her list of suspects.

As soon as Cheryl had run through the last of the formalities, she terminated the interview, thanked Malik for his time and escorted him back upstairs for one of the officers at the front desk to finish off before heading straight back down to see what Liberty had to say about things. Making her way into the observation room she was pleased to see that Liberty was still there in her wheelchair and promptly sat down as requested.

'You actually did very well, so don't go getting all

frustrated that you didn't get all the answers you'd hoped for. I've made notes for you to look over and think about a bit further, before getting back to me so we can discuss each point in detail. How does that sound?' Cheryl was more than pleased that Liberty had taken the time to do so, and was still busy thanking her as they made their way back up to the office.

'Oh, and by the way. I don't personally think Malik is the person we're after; although that's only my opinion and something you need to work out for yourself. Well done for today though Cheryl.' Those were the words of encouragement she loved hear as she watched Liberty wheeling her way towards Helen's desk before they headed off to the kitchen and disappeared from view.

*

Daniel Rosser had walked from the function room out into the corridor leading to the underground car park to have a sneaky cigarette despite having tried to give up for the third time that year. Social events always made him crave the old habit even more, and this time he could fight the urge no longer. There was a low noisy rumble of a motor as one of the lift generators kicked in and moved a few floors above. He assumed it was one of the security guards or a cleaner perhaps, but either way, he headed towards the car park. Just as he was approaching the door, a woman whom he took to be one of the waitresses passed close by, and then suddenly lurched straight into his side. In that instant, Daniel felt as if he'd been stung for a second. He suddenly came over all giddy, and then began struggling for breath as he moved sluggishly forward before coming to the top of the concrete stairs. As he peered down towards the bottom, it seemed to look a very long way down, and then the whole image started to swim around before his eyes. The next thing he knew, was that his legs had given way beneath him, the exact same time as he'd received a sharp shove in the back. The man was instantly launched headlong down the stairs, where his head struck something very hard just prior to everything going totally blank. Daniel Rosser never saw or heard the figure turn and leave the back of the building once they were satisfied with the end result. In fact, he never saw or heard anything ever again.

‎⁂

Mark was just lying on the bed staring up at the ceiling. He'd only just woken up with the duvet feeling damp from the terrible night he'd had, and his mind couldn't shake off the awful memories. In the silence, Mark could feel his heartbeat thumping away inside his chest and knew it was going far too fast. His whole body seemed to be filled with adrenaline, so much so, that it was almost like being high on drugs or one of those roller coaster rides that set you buzzing. In some respects, it was quite thrilling, but in others quite scary, but certainly not something he wanted to be feeling right now. What he felt was probably a throwback to when he'd been tortured by Langdon's men and left for dead in that godforsaken forest. Those were the images that kept coming back to haunt him and what he saw seemed so real at the time. It wasn't something that anyone who'd been through should ever have to suffer again.

 Despite all that had happened at the time, some of the images appeared to be embellished and grew ever gorier, with many ending ever so badly. This was what turned him from a happy, well respected young man into a miserable git just lately. The whole thing was squeezing in all around him, it felt very imposing and he didn't quite understand how Helen had put up with him for so long. She already had more than enough on her own plate without having to put up with his nonsense.

Mark thought back to the story she'd been telling him about the spate of murders linking back to the auditor with the flatmate who they felt may be the one doing the killings. It was only after he'd got up, showered, dressed then gone downstairs to have some breakfast that he came across the case file Helen had been working on. He couldn't help but have a look through and read up on some of the reports. It was human instinct as far as he was concerned, and although he knew he shouldn't be doing it, once he spotted the address, Mark felt it was a chance to redeem himself and do something useful for a change.

CHAPTER 9

The office car park covered a large space and was piled high with leaves as the autumn wind blew through the treetops bending the branches in all directions. The sky was a dismal grey which threw out a feeling of depressiveness and a stark reminder that winter was about to follow with another Christmas seemingly coming around so soon after the last one. The nights were already drawing in and Liberty just wanted to gather the information she wanted without any fuss. *Famous last words,* she thought, knowing damned well that something would crop up and take much longer than expected. This would leave her scrambling around in the dark trying to get back into her car without any lighting, as she hadn't noticed any on the way in, although the place seemed quite bare of other cars.

Liberty checked her watch and then took a deep breath as she wheeled herself through to the reception and stopped in front of the receptionist who seemed to look down at her with a fixed expression that had a slight hint of disapproval about it.

'You need to go downstairs to the car park. The other officers are already down there and you'll find two lifts just over there.' That was all she said to her as she pointed over to her left and then just carried on with something she was working on before Liberty's arrival. *'Not exactly the friendliest of welcomes I've ever had.'* Liberty thought as she wheeled across to where she'd indicated.

Liberty sat in the right-hand lift and waited patiently while it descended before announcing she'd reached the basement area in that robotic female voice which appeared in so many other electronic systems. *'She's certainly earned her dosh.'* Liberty thought again, as she prepared to wheel herself out onto the concrete surface that awaited her. The amount of room and the lighting was surprisingly very good and this explained why there were so few cars up top. Passing a couple of disabled bays, she realised her mistake and wondered if that was why the receptionist had been a bit off with her.

She'd come across DI David Manning before when he'd been the Senior Investigating Officer on another case that had been linked to one of hers a good few years ago. Some of his methods were known to be a little bit draconian at times, but many would say she wasn't any better. They both had a mutual respect for each other and both seemed to get the results that allowed them to get the job done, which was all that mattered at the end of the day. David wore an off-the-peg; high street suit that suited him quite well, although she knew he had more than enough money to afford something far more expensive if he wished. He was also a bit of a charmer who had the ability to turn it on and off at will, depending on the circumstances.

'So, what are we looking at here?' Liberty asked, once all the small talk was over.

'We've managed to identify the deceased as a Mr Daniel Rosser, a Financial Director in a company called Morotech Limited, which is based in this building here,' he told her.

'Apparently there was some sort of event held here last night, and that was the last time he was seen alive. Security has already checked the CCTV footage but nothing has shown up so far. There's also the added pain that there's more than a few other exits and entrances down here as well as the lifts. It's not a high security building so things tend to be pretty lax in general. I've already set my people on gaining statements from those who've shown up on the guest list, so we'll just have to wait to see if that throws up anything for now.'

They stood talking a bit longer while the forensics team finished doing what they needed to do with the body before one of the figures eventually broke away and walked towards them to break the news. Liberty recognised him as one of the team from the Richmond area, who she'd dealt with on two other occasions in the past. Donald Raggett reintroduced himself and told them to call him 'Don' as that was what everyone else did, apart from his wife, who he jokingly said called him all sorts of things. He commiserated with Liberty for ending up in a wheelchair and added that he'd heard about her misfortune through the police grapevine, which was sometimes more accurate than some of the communications published internally.

'It wasn't easy to spot at first, but I can confirm that the deceased had been injected in the neck before being pushed down the concrete stairs we found him at the bottom of. I'd estimate the time of death to be between eight and eleven o'clock last night at some time during the event that was going on up above. His neck was badly broken and there are various fragments of blood and bone on the edges of some of the stairs, which confirms he went down quite hard, at speed, and then tumbled quite a bit on the way down. The way he landed wasn't exactly graceful and the force with which he hit the concrete was adequate enough to fracture both the C1 and C2 vertebrae at the top of his neck. As you may or may not know, the human head can weigh between ten and thirteen pounds, so that would have made quite a sound for anyone to hear if they'd been passing by at the time. He wouldn't have stood much chance in all honesty, as these injuries are the most severe kind we find. A fall such as that would have caused immediate damage to the spinal cord and in doing so would have removed just about every ounce of communication to the rest of the body below that point. In this case it was fatal, which was probably best for him because if he'd lived, he'd have ended up fully paralyzed with an endless amount of neurological damage from the brain being without a blood source.' That was the point when Don suddenly realised what he'd said, went bright red in the face and apologised profusely to Liberty.

'For fuck's sake,' she exclaimed. Don't feel so bad around me. You're only telling it like it is, and that's what we need to know in this line of work. It's no use pussy footing around the truth just because I'm all trussed up like a turkey in this bloody wheelchair.' There was a distinct moment of silence before the three of them got back to what they were doing, with Don promising to give them the full report once the autopsy had been carried out.

*

Mark knew Helen wouldn't be best pleased if she discovered he'd started sticking his nose into her business, especially after everything that had happened with Bob Langdon and his crew. Helen had long laid down strict guidelines about interfering with each other's work, although she still tended to bounce ideas of him every now and again, especially when work started getting stressful or where she'd had a few drinks. Yet right now, although it was starting to get dark, she'd phoned to say she'd be working late at work, while he stood directly outside the large house in Chessington, having needed only one bus to reach the place. Mark stared up at the building that looked much larger than he'd expected it to be. As he waited and wondered what to do next, and feeling slightly stupid all of a sudden, he realised he could hear two raised voices coming from somewhere up above. It sounded like an argument was going on. One sounded male and the other female, so at that point he stepped back and looked up to see where the sound was coming from. From where he stood on the fully paved drive, Mark could just make out the edge of a roof terrace that was partially lit with two figures standing around on top. Not sure about what to do next, the decision was suddenly made up for him when one of the figures seemed to surge forward and scream as it dropped a bit then hung in mid-air screaming even louder. Mark frantically tried the front door but found it locked solid. Running around the side of the house he came across a side door which opened as soon as he tried the handle. Not wanting to waste a single second and without stopping for breath, he headed directly for the stairs and rushed up two at a time. Passing the second level, he then noted another set of stairs that he hoped would lead to the roof. Charging though the door at the top he suddenly found himself in a converted loft. The room was slightly unkempt with a single bed and a couple of computers lying around, but without stopping or bothering to pay too much attention to anything, Mark barged through and headed straight out onto the roof terrace.

Once there, Mark gazed over and tried to sum up the situation as fast as he could and work out how best to save the guy who now hung desperately clinging for life onto what looked like a broken railing and a bit of guttering with an extremely frightened look on his face. His worst fears were realised as he could see Malik's weight was seriously being tested right now. Just to add insult to injury there was a slight wind picking up with Mark hoping that the man's nerves would hold out. He really didn't want to join him if he fell to the concrete stretching out far below. Reaching over and doing his best to maintain his balance once he had a decent hold on a secure section of the roof, Mark grabbed at his free hand and managed to get a firm grip. The young man seemed to be much heavier than he first appeared.

'Don't look down and just think about how short the distance is to get back here. I'll count to three then on three I want you to kick yourself off that bit of brickwork that's situated just below your right foot. Ease down about an inch and you should feel it.' Mark watched as Malik did exactly that and then looked a little more confident before starting his count.

On three, Malik did just as he was told and Mark gave out a huge sigh of relief as he gained a tenuous grip on his upper arm as he flew towards him. Then, just as he was tightening his hold and about to pull Malik up, a darkened figure suddenly sprang from the inside of the house and barged straight into him. As Mark had been facing the other way, he had no chance to protect himself from the onslaught. Neither Mark nor Malik stood much chance of survival as they plunged the whole distance to the ground screaming. They'd stared into each other's eyes with a blatant expression of terror shared between them at one point during the fall, but the last few seconds shot past incredibly fast as both men landed heavily on the paved area below with pools of dark, crimson blood appearing beneath the badly crumpled bodies soon after. Malik had died instantly as he'd landed head first against the ground, Mark on the other hand had been more fortunate and still remained alive by some strange miracle.

Luckily, a neighbour passing by on her way home from work had heard the screams of both men and looked into the drive before dialling the emergency services on her mobile phone. Not that Mark was able to comprehend anything going on around him at that point.

*

The sun shone bright and strong in the sky as it beat down on those going about their everyday business. It felt unusually hot for this time of the year, but warmed Liberty's bones as she stole a glimpse down at her bare feet while walking through the grass in a large, spacious garden full of so many colourful flowers. Everything smelled wonderful at first. Then, she dared to take another look down and watched with great delight as each foot spread itself forward on a perfect green blanket of grass, while her weight gently shifted from one to the other without any difficulty.

As ever, the dream quickly dissipated as the alarm clock produced its annoying morning call, causing her head to become flooded with the latest cases she was working on.

'Damn it!' She uttered under her breath to no one but herself, as she automatically reached out to position her wheelchair in readiness for the busy day ahead. She knew it would be busy, as that was all it ever seemed to be nowadays. Life in general, ran at a hundred miles an hour and seemed to be the order of most people's days, especially for those she talked to in the force. Everything was running at pace, although in her case she guessed it could be seen as wheeling.

Crikey! She'd even woken up with a sense of humour for once. But how far would she get into the day before that all came crashing down? It wouldn't be too long.

*

Helen was beside herself when she'd first heard the news of what had happened. Malik had been confirmed dead at the scene and apparently Mark was in a bad way.

Mark! What the hell had he been doing there? Who the hell did he think he was, poking his face into something that was nothing to do with him?

Naturally, she was angry. The last time she'd stood over his hospital bed with the saline drip feeding all those drugs into his body to get the electrolytes back into his bloodstream and grown familiar with the machinery keeping him alive, hadn't exactly been fun. Her immediate action had been to confirm his condition with the doctors as soon as she'd arrived at the hospital, but now she felt incredibly nauseous when told he'd gone straight into surgery and she'd just have to be patient.

Patient! For fuck's sake, how much of that had she done in the past for that stupid, bloody boyfriend of hers? It was fair enough to say their relationship had become a bit strained recently, but this really did add the icing to the cake.

Helen was suddenly feeling extremely tired and pissed off, so it was perfect timing when Liberty wheeled herself up to where she stood and presented her with a much needed, much welcomed coffee.

Wiping away what she could of her tears, Helen eventually stopped pacing around the waiting area and took a seat beside her boss, who'd already pulled into a space at the end of the row. She was incredibly grateful that Liberty was beside her to help provide reassurance, yet deep inside her head, she knew it was different this time. It had been an absolute miracle he'd managed to survive the last time and been found in the forest. But how many chances did people get in life? According to the odds, he should now be lying flat on his back in cold storage with a bloodless face alongside Malik down in the morgue.

*

Helen's features tightened as she sat in familiar territory beside Mark's bed, not holding out much hope as she prepared for the worst based on what the doctors had said. Her eyes, already red and swollen from all the crying, switched across to the monitors working flat out to keep him alive. They then swopped to the copious amount of tubes attached to his bruised and broken body, only serving to confirm the fall from the roof terrace had done irreparable damage. Even if by some miracle Mark did pull through, she'd already been informed he'd be nothing more than a vegetable as the scans had shown very few traces of brain activity.

All she could think about was how crap their relationship had become just lately, especially in comparison to how loved up and happy they'd been in the past. Mark had never fully recovered from the torture he'd suffered at the hands of Langdon's thugs prior to being left for dead in that god forsaken forest. Helen was just sitting feeling sorry for herself when the audible alarm went off and the signal on the screen suddenly flatlined. The whole area filled with people in what seemed like a matter of seconds as a young male nurse escorted the distraught looking detective from the room and asked for her to wait outside.

*

Having Liberty beside her in her moment of need proved a great comfort to Helen. It was the not knowing that was so hard to bear, and it was just under an hour with yet another coffee polished off before the door opened up and the same male nurse walked in. He asked them to follow him into one of the side rooms and then told them the doctor would be with them very soon, ahead of departing to attend to someone else's needs. Helen felt as if the temperature around them had turned bitterly cold and instantly knew the news wouldn't be good. Sure enough, the news that finally followed, although expected, still came as an awful shock.

Later, as Liberty drove Helen back home, the two of them remained silent for most of the journey as Helen still couldn't speak through all the crying. Liberty knew she was angry at Mark, the force, and just about everything else that could be blamed for now. Helen would need a fair bit of support right now, and at least she'd agreed to sleep the night at Liberty's, once they'd stopped by her house to pick up a few things.

*

Feeling stressed and uptight inside with her mind racing ten to the gallon, Liberty pulled off the main road and stopped the car as she desperately needed a moment to herself. Pressing the button that wound the driver's side window down to allow her to breathe in some fresh air, she switched off the engine and sat in silence. Some of the thoughts she'd been having suddenly became a lot clearer as she looked up into the evening sky and marvelled at how red and spectacular it looked. 'Red sky at night, Shepherd's delight, red sky in the morning, Shepherd's warning.' She said out loud to herself. That was something her sister Susan always used to say when they were growing up together. She knew it had some sort of relationship to weather forecasting for sailor's way back in the past, but couldn't quite remember what it was exactly.

Liberty really missed her sister. Yet it was her murder at the hands of those crazy mixed up killers and others like them that really kept her going.

Suddenly, a slight shiver passed right though her. It was as if someone had just walked over her grave, yet Liberty simply sat where she was for a moment longer and realised how exhausted she felt. A gust of wind entered through the open window and whipped the left side of her hair into her face, but as she reached up to straighten it, it felt a little damp. At that point she realised she had tears in her eyes from thinking about Susan. It was still something quite raw in her mind, but she knew it would do her no good and needed to pull herself together. Right now, it was not all about her. This time it was Helen who needed her most, with Mark having just died a few days ago from his injuries.

How can some people be so unlucky in life? She wondered, taking in a few more deep breaths of fresh air before reaching towards the dashboard and restarting the engine. Liberty headed off towards Helen's place as she'd already decided to go back home.

As expected, there'd be some sort of enquiry held as to why the railing on the roof terrace had been unsafe in the first place and the landlord would no doubt be prosecuted in some way, although that would still be far too late to help out Mark or Malik or those grieving their passing.

CHAPTER 10

It was starting to grow dark in the skies above as night gradually began to draw in and put an end to yet another day. Rob Winter, an ex-soldier whose wife had also served in the forces but been killed in an explosion during her service, gave the boat a bit of extra speed as he knew only too well that he needed to find a mooring for the night; seeing as the last place had been full up with people who'd arrived earlier than him. The whole canal had become so much busier over the last few years with people looking to find what they hoped would be somewhere cheaper to live. Rented accommodation and house prices were continuously rising and showed absolutely no sign of easing up.

Rob had left the rat race six years earlier despite having had a go at running a warehouse for a medium sized electronics company as well as needing to come to terms with the hardship and emotions of being on his own. The idea of being his own boss and tying his brightly painted boat in by the likes of a marina in a town or city centre or alongside a meadow or a field was far more attractive with fewer restrictions involved.

It was like choosing whatever scenery or backdrop you fancied having each day to suit your mood in conjunction with the seasons and weather conditions at each time of the year. It was an idyllic lifestyle, although it still had its hardships and protocols just like everything else. Having food, the correct facilities and services were essential but life on the canal was something you had to learn to adapt to pretty fast or you wouldn't last too long. Lack of moorings was definitely the biggest problem at this point in time, but just then, as he approached and then negotiated the next bend in the canal, a smile suddenly lit up his whole face as he recognised the red brick apartments looming up just ahead in the distance.

As he moved closer on the steady current with his engine ticking over, not wishing to create too big a wash, the light and reflections from the apartment windows spilled onto the water and confirmed the fact there was a vacant space available with plenty of room for him to manoeuvre his thirty-one foot trailerable narrowboat into position between two others that looked to be slightly larger than his. Rob was looking forward to settling down for the night and wondered what his new neighbours would be like or if he'd recognise them from a previous meeting? Not that you always met them, especially as so many boats were hired out or just used for weekends.

*

Visiting officers were also allowed hot desk facilities as their office had four spaces that housed everything they would need to just dock their laptops and connect to the intranet via a protected Wi-Fi as well as accessing the Holmes database if needed. Most officers preferred to work surrounded by a team rather than being left out on their own. Liberty could only think of a couple who preferred otherwise, and both of those were coming up to retirement fairly soon.

Liberty spent the next few hours studying CCTV footage of the Thamesdale industrial estate and then realised it was fast approaching ten o'clock before deciding it would be best to call it a day. She'd intended to leave a lot earlier, but time had just flown by without her even noticing. She still required quite a bit of background information for what she needed to focus in on, but she knew she wouldn't be able to get that until the next morning when Cheryl was back in work.

Once she was finally back at home, having had a bit of trouble with her wheelchair, due to a piece of chewing gum that some selfish dickhead had spat out without a single thought for anyone else, she decided that having had a quick sandwich at lunchtime with Helen at her home had been sufficient enough. She really couldn't be arsed to cook so late in the evening anyway. Thankfully, it also looked like Helen would be back to work sooner rather than later, having been told officially to take her allowance and use it to grieve. Liberty knew only too well how hard it was. She'd definitely sensed her partner itching to get back on the job when she'd been there with her.

Wheeling herself into the bedroom, and having checked her phone for any missed calls; of which there were none, Liberty felt a desperate urge to grab a bit of a sleep. Without even bothering to undress, she manoeuvred herself across and onto the duvet with practiced ease before laying back and closing her eyes. Thankfully, the blackout backing to her curtains worked their magic by blocking out the annoying light she used to get off the streetlight that lived right outside. It wasn't long before the DCI was fast asleep in the land of nod with the hope she wouldn't suffer one of those horrible reoccurring dreams.

*

As the businessman worked his way home and picked his usual route along a narrow pathway next to the canal, a rather ominous looking figure remained hidden in the shadows just ahead. Having reached into their pocket and withdrawn the pre-prepared hypodermic syringe which was fully loaded and ready for use, they performed a quick check by tapping it a few times to make sure there were no bubbles present.

 As the target drew closer, totally unaware of the danger because he was so engrossed in what was happening on his Smartphone and unable to hear anything from listening to music through a set of white earphones, the killer darted out from behind as soon as the man had gone past. Jamming the needle into the victim's neck, Andrew Morrison buckled at the knees and went down as a strange numbness suddenly flooded his body while the chemical reaction worked pretty damn fast. The initial pain he'd felt had turned scorching hot in an instant. It felt like a bad sting or possibly a burn from a burning poker before the lack of any sensation kicked in and took full effect. If he'd expected the feeling to subside, Andrew had got it badly wrong as the figure edged him towards the water with the businessman discovering he was completely unable to react.

 Unbeknown to him, Andrew Morrison had been a subject recently talked about just prior to Malik's death. Mike had been nattering on about him to his housemates one evening because the guy had been such a prat at a past audit. It was only as he'd driven past a certain supermarket chain of the same name that he'd recalled how the guy had acted at the time and decided to bring it up in conversation.

*

The whole stretch of canal had been running clear for a good long while with no sign of any boats either in front or behind him. There had been one short section a while back where he'd had to slow down for some moored boats, which was all part of the code of behaviour that needed to be followed on the waterways, but that hadn't been a problem and he'd soon been back up to normal speed. The ex-soldier, Rob Winter had studied the canal guide for this section and knew there was a fairly decent run before the next lock would start to appear in the distance. Adding more power by pushing the throttle back further, the boat gradually picked up a bit more speed while Rob made sure he kept a close eye on the wash behind him to guarantee he wasn't going too fast and creating much of a wake. The plant life on the riverbanks was interspersed with so many variations of bushes and trees that there was always something ready to catch the eye. Reeds soared and swayed majestically in the breeze and ducks rushed out from undercover every now and again as they waited expectantly for bits of bread to be fed to them. Sometimes they'd return without a single morsel, although there'd be plenty of other occasions where they'd end up pigging out on a generous handful, especially where kids were usually involved on the larger family sized boats that passed by.

Herons could be seen in the far distance every now and again, looking like statues most of the time, yet nine times out of ten they'd always launch themselves up into the air just seconds before any boat drew even with them. Their long, sticklike legs would simply fold back just like the undercarriage of a large aeroplane taking off from a runway. This was what allowed them to look so amazingly graceful as they flew low and followed the long line of water for a distance before coming to rest a little further along. They'd then repeat the whole process all over again once the boat approached again. It was a game these magnificent creatures just loved to play and their patience as they scanned the water would eventually be rewarded with a fish in the end.

Rob had been very fortunate as the day had proved to be a good one weather-wise. There'd still been a pleasant breeze blowing and it had been ever so refreshing with the sun doing its best to cook the inhabitants both in and out of the water. All sorts of sounds from the canal, be it wildlife, other boats, chatter from passersby on the paths or noises from the roads and railway lines had become far too familiar. So much so, that most of them just blended into the background and were usually taken for granted. Time drifted by for Rob as the day passed ever onwards and acted as a reminder of why he loved this lifestyle so much, having chosen to live this way following the misfortune of being wounded in action during his service in the middle east and ending up with an artificial limb.

Having been in such a relaxed state of mind, it therefore came as a complete shock when he rounded the next corner and saw what looked to be a person being pushed without a struggle into the canal. This was being carried out by a hooded figure who then turned and shot off onto a pathway surrounded by a large profusion of trees and hedges that completely hampered his view. With the boat already moving as fast as It would allow, and knowing it was far too far to swim, Rob headed directly toward the spot in the distance where the figure had gone under a short while earlier. He guided the vessel with great expertise, despite feeling sick inside and not knowing what he'd be likely to find once he eventually got there.

*

Cheryl was taking in everything Liberty was saying. These were the golden moments when it was so important to listen and soak up everything being said. These things didn't tend to come around all that often and were so important to officers like her, who still had most of their working lives ahead of them. Being taught about murder investigations in the academy was one thing, but learning on the job was much more useful. Liberty had explained how young children were capable of so much more with regard to innovation as their minds were still open to just about any possibility until adults came along and told them they needed to conform to what we saw as the norm, which then ruined their ability to think outside the box. Liberty was sharing that fact because casting all the crap from her mind and looking at the crime scene with no preconceived ideas or expectations was what worked for her. It was something she'd picked up in her earlier days in the force, and had certainly been something that had paid out a good few dividends so far.

'You need to work fast and completely absorb your surroundings before placing that image firmly in your mind then moving on and tracing the rest. The art of recalling such details could prove to be the make or break in some cases, and that's something anyone can condition their brain to do if it doesn't come naturally.'

Liberty was well aware she had a captive audience as she commanded instant respect from the confines of her wheelchair, knowing she'd have been just as a tentative if the tables had been turned many years earlier.

'Many of those first impressions will be no use at all, but you may get a gut feeling about something that you can't quite put your finger on that could turn up trumps later, although that's usually when you're least expecting it. So, think back to where we are right now with our needle killer, then try to work out if there's anything stored away in your grey matter that might prove useful.'

Liberty had already covered the sad news about Andrew Morrison's death in the canal at the start of the talk, so decided to leave it at that for now. She could see for herself that some of what she'd just said had hopefully sunk in and would provide some decent afterthought.

'Okay! The team talk's over, so now let's get back to work and come up with the goods. No pressure anyone. I know you all understand that at least.' Liberty also had to bring it to an end because they had another one of those damned press conferences to cover.

*

It was good to be back sitting with both feet firmly planted under her desk again. Helen turned the moment she realised someone was behind her. She'd half expected that person to be Liberty and was obviously very pleased once that was confirmed.

As ever, Helen's long, shapely, olive coloured legs stretched out before her and this beautiful young woman, who'd now been her partner for a decent time just never seemed to get any older despite all the shit she'd just been through yet again.

'Anything I need to be aware of at the moment?'

'No boss.' Helen replied. 'Although grabbing a coffee wouldn't be too much to ask right now, would it?'

'No, I guess not.' Liberty shot back. 'Let's head for Jean's Café. That's on the way to where we need to go to next, with the added bonus that I can fill you in with some of the finer details regarding where we are at the moment. I think I told you most things when I last popped in to see you at home, but let's do it anyway. Come on, grab your coat and I'll race you to the lift.'

Helen laughed as she did as she was told. She knew Liberty was finding life in a wheelchair pretty hard at times, but she never ever showed it unless she was really struggling with something.

*

Tom could find Jenny incredibly moody now and then. Sometimes she'd drive him absolutely mad, especially when she behaved like a sulky child. Yet those would be the moments when he'd ask what the hell he was still doing with her, putting up with so much crap. Likewise, when she was in a good mood, life could be incredibly exciting, plus there was the fact that she fucked like a rampant rabbit, which was certainly one of the more positive points to their odd relationship. Jenny was what he'd have referred to as a bit of a 'wild child' at one time, and despite having been together for a good while now, he sure as hell didn't know that much about her. She never talked about her past and he really didn't have a clue as to whether she had any family to speak of or not. To say Jenny was a little bit strange would certainly have been an understatement, yet in his own way, Tom also respected her privacy and fully agreed that she was well within her own rights to do as she pleased. Maybe one day she'd decide to open up to him, but again that was something he wasn't willing to push too far. He knew deep down that would be a sure-fire way of losing her completely. That definitely wouldn't be something worth chancing, especially considering the amount of trust they'd managed to build up during their time together. At least that was how he viewed things for the moment.

The dining table in the back room where'd they'd sat and eaten together still had their cups and plates on it with Jenny's half eaten sandwich still looking reasonably edible. Tom stared out of the patio windows and watched the local fox with its white ended tail climb down from the back fence. It then stood and then gazed around with a somewhat guilty expression on its face. At least that was his interpretation from where he sat feeling quite pissed off right now.

For some bizarre reason Jenny had just grabbed the old army jacket she'd bought from a charity shop and then shot off without even having the courtesy to tell him where she was off to. That just about summed up exactly how the woman was behaving at present and what really frustrated him was that she chose to be so bloody secretive about everything.

He remembered the time that they'd first met. She'd been in a hurry and looking quite flustered when they'd collided together as they'd both been trying to escape the mad rush in the underground station at the same time. He'd been really surprised when she'd said yes to his offer of buying her a drink to apologise at one of the local pubs. So, the fact that she'd ended up at his place for the night and then tried to fuck his brains out was a total revelation to both his own esteem and his cock, which admittedly, had looked a little worse for wear the next day.

The woman had been totally insatiable under the covers. It had seemed as if she'd needed someone like him to protect her at times, yet they'd remained a couple ever since. Another odd thing was she'd never explained where she'd been living. Wherever it was, she must have returned. He realised that because she'd turned up the next day with a small rucksack that he'd not seen before, and even that contained very few possessions compared to most of the women he'd known. He'd therefore assumed that Jenny wasn't very materialistic and just preferred to travel light so hadn't thought much more about it at the time.

Now, staring down at his watch, Tom decided he may as well clear the table then nip out to get some milk as he knew they were getting a bit low. Likewise, it would also give him something to do and hopefully force his mind to switch onto something else for a change.

CHAPTER 11

Liberty allowed her eyes to wander across the screen and take in the information being provided. Only a small percentage was likely to come in useful but she'd always proved very perceptive and her mind genuinely had a knack of storing large chunks of data and being able to recall certain things that had proved useful in the past. Just then, she heard someone behind her make a noise that was obviously intended to capture her attention. Pushing back from the desk and swivelling her wheelchair around to face the person in question, Liberty smiled up at Helen who'd simply walked over to remind her she had a meeting with Heather in two minutes time.

*

Sitting directly in front of her boss, Liberty sat and listened very carefully.

'The next meeting with those mindless gannets from the press really needs to go well. They're constantly on our backs right now, especially when things take so much longer than expected and then another body decides to go and turn up in the canal. We need to fully emphasise this isn't as straightforward a case as some of the others we've dealt with in the past. They need to remain patient and allow us to exercise our rights to deal with this case undisturbed, at our own pace and in our usual professional manner, if you please'.

Liberty could clearly sense Heather was doing her best to remain calm even though she knew her to be under a great deal of pressure from above. Unfortunately, this tactic of affirming the case as being more complex would no doubt raise the level of curiosity amongst many of the reporters, but hopefully it would also provide them with a greater level of credit once the whole thing was finally solved and put to rest.

'Oh! There's one more thing'. Heather added, lowering her voice. 'That case regarding the warehouse at the Thamesdale sounds like it's about to heat up a lot more. I'll let you know as soon as anything's confirmed, but start getting the team ready anyway. You choose who you want, but it may be useful if you take the two newbie's along to get a feel for what it's really like out there when things go down.

*

Just as Liberty was steering her wheelchair out of the office, she started pondering about their whole relationship with the press. Why was it the media always seemed to hold the upper hand the majority of the time? There were always plenty of stories out there for them to get their teeth into, such as the recent school shootings in America where a large number of students had died or the man who'd murdered his wife and kids before killing himself in a village just outside Reading. This would always be followed up with examples of mental health problems that countries faced, yet still seemed to do very little about it. Likewise, the pages of newspapers and TV coverage would tend to focus in on gun control and question why in this day and age a so-called forward-thinking country like the states still preferred its citizens to be armed. There'd been a large fire at some historic site in London's city centre and some big sleazy scandal going on within the government as well as the death of a really well-known British film star who was a complete legend in most households. Yet the minute there was the slightest whiff of police corruption, the press would descend like a pack of vultures wanting to know every single detail. In such cases, the force would be busy carrying out numerous internal investigations whilst trying their best to avoid any possible leaks. That only added to the pressure and made life harder than it ever needed to be for everyone, which really didn't help those who just wanted to get on and deliver a decent days work.

*

'I've got something in my head that's been bugging me for a long time now.' Liberty drew the team's attention to the picture board. They'd already adjusted it to a lower position to allow her to move a few photo's around to suit her needs.

'I think we've all fallen for something linked to our personal comfort zones way of thinking. Just try and get your heads around the idea that our killer is acting a bit like a chameleon and has the ability to change things around so we're now looking the wrong way. Then add in the idea that this person may well have been there all along, but we just hadn't noticed them.'

Cheryl Burgess had her hand raised and was already demonstrating she was not only good, but fitting into the team much faster than Luke King was. She was the one who'd have no difficulty in speaking her mind, while he was much shyer and tended to be quite laid back.

'Everyone in this room has been desperately working their socks off on this case, especially after I'd informed Helen she needed to take a break following Mark's death.' Liberty continued.

All eyes turned to Helen who sat quietly at the back of the room for now. It was evident they were glad to have her back, but she was also very interested to hear what Cheryl had to say, especially as Liberty had previously informed her she was the one to watch.

'So, what's your particular reasoning on this one then?'

Liberty sat in her wheelchair and looked straight across at Cheryl as she waited at the front of the room. She liked this woman and had a good feeling that she'd be going places, sooner rather than later. Cheryl stood and spoke with great confidence.

'Well our first victim was Jared Boyle in the shopping mall which was swiftly followed by David Boston on a train. Lorraine Carey was next in the design company's car park with Daniel Rosser in another, albeit that that was an underground one. Then more recently, Andrew Morrison turned up in the canal, and although it sounds like they weren't the nicest bunch of business people you'd ever wished to have met, they still didn't deserve what happened to them.

All of these cases led us to Mike Britton as being the prime suspect as he'd audited the victim's businesses at some time prior to their murders, yet as soon as it became quite clear it wasn't him and looked to be his flatmate Malik, it all looked as if it would be plain sailing after that. Sadly, he's now ended up being murdered, which naturally shifts him from being the prime suspect to yet another murder victim.'

The team all sat listening and although impressed with Cheryl's self-assurance, most of them wondered where exactly this was going next.

'So, let's just take a moment to step outside the box and look once again at what we've been left with. Following Malik's death, I guess we all assume the killer must still be associated to the house in some way. Yet what if they may not necessarily be a housemate any longer, or what if the killer just happens to be female?' There were a few intakes of breath at that point so Cheryl stopped what she was saying and looked around to gain the teams reactions before continuing. 'So how does that now change the game and who does the finger of possibility point to?' There was finally a lot more noise following her last statement, but she decided it best to carry on while she still had a captive audience.

'I suggest we focus on our little miss innocent, Jenny Manson and see what comes up. We certainly have nothing to lose at the moment.'

Those seated around had mixed emotions with some even starting to discuss this suggestion with their colleagues as the whole room suddenly started to spring to life once again. A couple of others stared into space as they sat and considered what had just been said a little bit further, while Cheryl simply sat back down and congratulated herself on having had the desired affect she'd set out to create in the first place.

Liberty allowed a few minutes for things to be processed then wheeled herself to the front and took over once again. Thanking Cheryl for her thoughts and having shared them openly with the team, she added a few more announcements then finally dismissed the meeting having asked the team to see what they could come up with as a follow up to this latest idea.

*

The tip about the warehouse raid had come in two days earlier, so the crack team had been well prepared and ready to go once they were given the green light. Having got wind of what was going on, Liberty had pulled a few strings to allow two members of her team to go along to get a bit more front-line experience. It hadn't been easy, but at least she'd won out in the end. That was why Cheryl Burgess and Luke King now sat inside the back of the speeding van all geared up with their cell phones turned off as instructed.

The last time they'd both worn bullet-proof vests had been back during their police training. That hadn't been too long ago, but it still seemed like an age away. Cheryl had forgotten how heavy they were and how much it would make her shoulders ache for the next few days. Both she and Luke were feeling pretty anxious but were glad that Liberty had given them something to get involved in rather than having them sitting behind their computer screens for a change. She was a good boss and they knew they'd learnt a lot from working in her team so far.

Knowing that if everything was going according to plan, they'd soon be at the warehouse, Cheryl gazed over at Luke and could see quite clearly just how nervous he was. They'd both been given solid briefings on the plans. It had been three times over in order to ensure they were fully aware of how things were going to be carried out, but the golden rule was they were only there to observe. The squad they were riding with had an incredibly dangerous job to do and there was no room for mistakes. This remark had been especially aimed at the two of them, as the others wouldn't have time to babysit them along the way.

These were the professionals. It went without saying that they knew exactly what to look for, and were damned good at it.

Once they'd finally arrived, the doors were thrown wide open with Cheryl and Luke getting a clear view of the enormous warehouse they were about to enter. Cheryl stared with unease at the place and felt a horrible lump suddenly appear in her throat. This was a warning sign that had sprung up inside her many times before, and it always told her something bad was about to happen.

'Hang on a minute.' She said, grabbing hold of Luke by the arm with more force than she'd meant to use. 'Let's be careful and not do anything stupid. We're only here to watch this operation, not to take part. We need this to run smoothly because we'll both find it impossible to live with ourselves if anything goes wrong, or if anyone gets hurt due to something we've done.

Sure enough, deep inside the warehouse, four men armed with guns equipped with silencers and dressed in dark clothing were spotted moving cautiously up and down the aisles looking for something in particular. Two security guards lay unconscious back in the office where they'd both been overpowered and given a good beating. The men who'd attacked wearing face masks were extremely vicious and had no qualms whatsoever about killing someone if they were forced to do so. Cheryl thought she could hear their whispers at one time, but knew that that couldn't be true from that distance, although it could have been put down to the steel frame of the warehouse acting like some sort of echo chamber. The main part of the police squad had already headed off at great speed into the central area where they knew the robbers would be. Cheryl and Luke were effectively bringing up the rear with their guide and therefore, according to theory, it would all be done and dusted by the time they'd eventually caught up with them.

The first four aisles they passed had proved to be clear apart from a forklift truck that had sat inactive in the darkness of the third one. The racking had orange steel frames that reached right up to the vaulted ceiling high above. Cheryl counted six levels in total and was quite amazed at how full each shelf appeared to be. Apparently this was a very busy building in the day time and although most of the stock was deemed to be low cost with high volume sales, there was a certain area that held some very specialist equipment which was worth a whole lot more. That was supposed to be a well-kept secret, but it had obviously leaked out to the wrong people at some time.

Just as they were drawing closer to the middle of the warehouse, Cheryl jumped as the sound of gunfire echoed around the building and sounded a lot louder than it would outside. Luke snapped his head around and looked to see if she was okay before deciding to poke his face around the next corner to gain a better look.

It later turned out to have been a freak accident that had occurred at that exact same moment, with Luke's legs suddenly buckling and his body going completely limp. A stray bullet from one of the robber's guns had taken Luke right between the eyes and killed him instantly. Cheryl managed to get a facial of warm blood along with bits of brain matter all over her. How she didn't scream or panic right there and then was a tribute to her bravery and teaching. Quite a few stray bullets had torn through parts of the warehouse during the moment the robbers had been overpowered. Everything had gone according to plan up to that point, it was only Sod's law that had kicked in and ruined everything by ensuring it went wrong with one of the worst possible outcomes.

*

Liberty sat in the shade under a tree in her wheelchair in the little park located just across the road from the station. She was busy studying the gardens that had suffered more than their fair share of vandalism in the past from local kids who always claimed they were innocent whenever they'd been caught doing something untoward. The sun was beaming down from behind and hitting an exposed section on the back of her neck, although it wasn't yet hot enough to leave a tan, as it was still early spring. Her attention was fixed on a young squirrel that was attempting to tackle a large pizza box that had been dumped in one of the litter bins. It was proving quite comical as the box seemed to be protecting what she assumed to be a piece of pizza stuffed inside. Yet something seemed to be holding it in and the DCI laughed inwardly at the poor tormented creature's fearless attempts at winning its prize. She'd really needed something like that to take her mind off the death of Luke King. His shooting had really cut up the whole team who were understandably feeling extremely down right now. Sleep would have been another useful thing for them all to have, but she doubted any of them were able to get much of that at the moment, especially with all the shit coming down from above as well as that of the media.

Her mind had just been wondering off to explore another thought when a pair of feet suddenly appeared in her line of sight and someone stood purposely in front of her. A smile then crossed Liberty's face as she recognised the fancy shoes.

'Heather,' she greeted the figure, as she looked up and wondered if she should mention anything about Luke.

'Morning Liberty," Heather replied politely. 'Did you get any sleep at all last night?'

'No, of course not, and I can't imagine you did either.' she responded, with her tone sounding slightly apprehensive.

Heather shrugged. Her head hung down and she looked drawn as she sat down on the nearby bench Liberty had wheeled across to. She'd soon followed close behind once she'd realised what her DCI was about to do.

'I'm sorry Heather. I know this isn't easy for you.' Liberty said softly. 'It's hard for me and the team to come to grips with too. Yet it's you who seems to take the flack every time something like this goes down.' she affirmed with an obvious expression of concern stretched across her face.

'It's not the first time and it won't be the last unfortunately. You know as well as I that it comes with the job. However, regardless of what's happened, I still want you to let me get on with the political crap alongside the ten ton of red tape that's involved. I've already had a meeting with Luke's family but what I need you and the team to do right now is to get some damned answers so we can take some of the heat off.'

Liberty felt a deep sense of frustration and despaired for her boss's current predicament. She then took a big deep breath before promising her boss they'd do everything possible. Liberty knew she really didn't have to justify anything as Heather knew they were already working flat out and busting a gut to do so. Heather stood then placed her hand on Liberty's shoulder before saying anything further.

'I have things that need to get sorted rather urgently. I'll get off now and leave you to manage things the way you know best. Good luck Lib's and don't hold back if you need to come to me for anything.'

What she'd said was certainly from the heart and Liberty didn't have a single shred of doubt about her boss meaning what she'd just said. There was a genuine bond that held them all together and her intentions were always sincere, especially after all the shit they'd been through in the past.

Liberty sat and watched her go before deciding she'd better get off herself as she placed her arms in position to enable the wheelchair to set off.

CHAPTER 12

Sitting down on the edge of her bed she stared down at the fine hairs showing on the front of her long, shapely legs. They stood out from the way the light reflected on them and it seemed as though they almost had a mind of their own as each follicle poked up and desperately called for attention. In a natural reaction, Jenny reached down and started to scratch away with both hands working a leg each. She scratched casually at first and it felt really pleasant, but then she upped the pace with her hands working faster with the pressure on her legs increasing. Without even thinking about what she was doing, a red mist started to descend as the young woman continued to scratch away and gain an increasing feeling of pleasure. Scratching harder and harder with her sharp uneven nails, the skin beneath them finally gave way as she punctured the outer surface and released small trenches of blood that appeared in the gouges and trickled down to the floor. As she grew more elated and got caught up in the whole euphoria, Jenny lost all sense of her surroundings as her mind drifted back to a moment in time that still haunted her to that very second. Focusing back to the vision of her mother sitting trapped and helpless in the burning car when she'd been a young girl with so much to live for, Jenny recalled all she'd been able to do was watch and stare with helpless abandon as the flames licked around the struggling figure inside. Yet even as her hair caught alight and the screams became unbearable to listen to, there had still been a macabre fascination about the whole thing. The sound of her mother's pain and suffering had been almost inhuman and not something a child of her age should ever have been exposed to. It was no wonder she now had so many issues to deal with, despite the fact she'd hidden them so well and managed her lifestyle the way she'd wanted.

Once the image faded away and Jenny's mind finally settled back in the real world, the woman managed to regain her focus and felt pain. She felt the heat throbbing away in her legs then sat all wide eyed and almost out of breath from the effort she'd put in. Gazing down she squirmed as she saw her legs had become a bloody mess and she'd really fucked them up big time. Getting to her feet and walking slowly across to the battered chest of drawers up against the far wall, she rummaged through the contents and grabbed out a pair of black jeans before making her way out to the bathroom. Jenny needed to clean herself up and change into something that wouldn't show up what she'd done to herself. Luckily, fortune was on her side for a change as she stepped from the room with the rest of the house remaining silent, which meant the small talk she'd already half prepared wasn't needed. There were moments when Jenny genuinely liked being in the midst of other people, but occasions like this were definitely not classed as one of those times.

As she stepped into the kitchen, she couldn't help but notice the newspaper lying open on the table. The heading about Andrew Morrison's body in the nearby canal instantly caught her eye and on reading the item she realised the witness on the houseboat could prove to be a big problem for her. Committing the name Rob Winter and the name of his boat to memory, Jenny realised he'd still be likely to be in the area as the police would want him to remain close by until things were sorted out. Sorting him out was exactly what she had in mind as she started devising a rough plan, grabbed what she needed and promptly left the house after swiping a banana that was staring to turn brown in the fruit bowl before leaving.

*

Doing just as the police had asked by staying put in case they had any further questions; Rob had eaten locally but now decided to leave the warmth of the waterside pub. It had proved to be extremely pleasant and a great venue for drinks with a wide choice of menus and great offers of fresh food with daily specials displayed on the in-house chalk board. Of course, that had made choosing what to eat much harder, but it had lots of friendly staff to help him decide. There was also a fantastic outside seating area he'd passed on the way in, which looked perfect for an al fresco lunch in the summertime with Rob feeling quite tempted to return at some time in the future.

Once outside, he looked up at the sky to check out what was happening as it had turned out to be quite a nice night. It had literally stopped raining when he'd first stepped into the place, although he hadn't been very wet, which may have had something to do with the umbrella he'd remembered to take along. It had only been a typical shower that you'd expect around that time of the year, while the sun had been doing its best to poke its face through the clouds at the time.

Now it was close to ten-thirty in the evening, much darker than when he'd first set off. The moon shone majestically amongst the stars above and the lights dotting that section of the canal path were in full flow as it was closer to town and a fairly busy section popular with joggers, dog walkers and commuters who preferred walking to work. It was fairly empty now however, as most people would have long gone home to wherever their lives had taken them. Yet for some strange reason, as he walked back to his houseboat, Rob detected an unusual sensation of fear hanging in the air that made him feel slightly uneasy and a little on edge. His instincts usually tended to be pretty good, especially as he'd relied on them so much during his days in the armed forces. Therefore, he was more than a little anxious to find out what the hell was causing it. The man shivered despite the fact it still remained a fairly warm night, and he couldn't wait to be clear of the place as he checked out his surroundings with greater caution than usual as he continued to walk along.

Taken completely by surprise once he'd reached the boat and stepped on board with everything looking to be fine, Rob was far too slow to react for a change. He'd glimpsed something sharp and shiny moving towards him out of the corner of his eye, but it was literally pure luck that it just happened to kiss the side of his face as he'd been about to descend the steps into the cabin. He heard the frustration of whoever it was that attacked him and should really have been ready for the kick that caught him on the back of the head just a split second later. That sent him flying down the stairs before landing in a rather undignified heap whilst catching his elbow on the side of the hardwood table in trying to cushion his fall. Rob automatically put his hand up to his cheek to check out his facial wound before discovering the tiny amount of blood meant it was only a superficial cut. In that same instant the attacker panicked then drove the weapon into the lower section of his left leg. There was obviously an element of surprise when he was still able to move without seeming to be disabled in any way, and this caused the figure to turn and flee back up the stairs without question.

Rob heard a loud splashing sound as he finally pulled his senses together, got to his feet and set off up the stairs in pursuit. Standing on the front deck of the boat, he watched helplessly as the attacker had already cleared the distance across to the other side of the canal and was already climbing up onto the bank. They'd been wearing some sort of old camouflaged army jacket that must have been quite hard to swim in as well as keeping their shoes on. Yet, there was something about the way the figure moved in the distance and behaved during the attack that wasn't quite right to him. This set Rob thinking about what it could be, and then it instantly started to nag at him. Already aware there was no point in pursuing the figure, Rob shouted out how he felt before watching the attacker finally run off up the path and completely disappear from view.

Rob eventually headed back down the steps, closed the hatch doors for the night, and then rang the number on the card he'd been handed by the female DCI. As he started to make the call, Rob stared down at the needle still sticking out of the prosthetic leg that began just below his left knee. He couldn't help but laugh out loud as he realised just how lucky he must have been before deciding he'd best leave the needle where it was for the police to see for themselves.

*

Sitting together in Jean's Café, their favourite coffee haunt which also served as a much-needed bolt hole from all the craziness, was well overdue. Zoe and her staff were always on hand to help Liberty set up her wheelchair by moving tables and chairs around without any problem.

Following a short wrangle over whose turn it was to pay for the drinks with Helen standing around having won, then having waited for Alex, the new employee to return her credit card, she eventually walked back across to Liberty. They readily chatted away, as this was their first real chance to stop and catch up with each other since the interview earlier in the day with Rob Winter on his houseboat by the canal. They'd rushed to see him as soon as Liberty had received the call, yet they'd both been totally blown away at the sight of him just sitting there with the needle still poking out of his leg. The guy obviously had a sense of humour despite the attempt on his life by a person's unknown. Rob talked with a great deal of clarity and his description of what had happened was incredibly detailed. The way he said it also made it very easy to picture exactly what had gone on. Likewise, his gut-feeling of something he couldn't quite put his finger on at the time had been given a decent amount of breathing space while he'd waited for the two women to arrive, and this left the man ninety-nine percent sure that his attacker had been a female. It was either that or a very effeminate male. He'd also provided a good description of what the attacker had been wearing, which was always useful as something extra to go on. The bit of fabric that looked to be a section of pocket from the jacket the attacker had been wearing had been instantly bagged up for forensics to have a look at.

A brisk walk over to the far bank where the figure had fled hadn't provided any clues from what the two of them could see. Likewise, forensics had been phoned and asked to visit and have a look over the area too. Sadly, they were already working flat out and didn't feel the chances of finding anything would prove very successful. They'd stated the fact that it was on a very busy footpath and combined with it having rained quite heavily since then; really didn't help. Naturally, this placed the visit much lower down on their list of priorities, and there wasn't a great deal that either of them could do about it, which proved extremely frustrating.

Liberty took a long deliberate swig of her coffee before bringing that very point up with her partner. She knew Helen would not only be very interested in what she was about to say, but would no doubt be thinking along exactly the same lines already. They stopped mid-conversation for a moment or two, while a young mother with a pram tried to negotiate her way to the door. This involved Liberty's wheelchair having to be manoeuvred over to the side just slightly in order for her to reach the exit. However, once they'd finally resettled and got back to the point in question, they both agreed that Cheryl's theory of it being a female killer actually made much more sense now.

If she'd been right about that, then her remark about focusing on Jenny Manson as the little miss innocent housemate was really worth pursuing. For that very reason alone, that was what remained the main topic of discussion for the rest of their time spent in Jean's Café.

'So, let's get straight onto this young lady and see what comes up. We've nothing better to go on right now, so we really don't have anything to lose.' Liberty had declared.

Now she had Helen's full backing on that being the best way to proceed, they both agreed this could turn out to be a very interesting path to take. Hopefully, and with wishful thinking, this would prove to be the breakthrough they so needed right now.

As they drained the remnants of their well-earned cappuccinos with the two empty plates beside them displaying nothing more than a few crumbs from the 'naughty cakes' as they'd referred to them earlier; Zoe spotted Helen start to stand up and promptly rushed over to help. The two female detectives, who she always found to be more than interesting in more ways than one, bade their farewells to just about everyone sitting around before leaving.

Zoe stood and peered out the window whilst watching their progress and wondering what they'd be getting up to next. Helen wheeled Liberty off towards the big black car parked just outside. This was the only available disabled parking space and it couldn't have been situated in a better position.

Maybe that was another reason why Jean's Café was the perfect choice.

*

136

Jenny was so annoyed with the way things had turned out. She'd thought the guy would be some kind of softie nature lover because he lived on the canal, but he'd certainly known how to handle himself, as she'd just discovered to her detriment. She'd made the fatal mistake of assuming something instead of finding out the full facts first. She couldn't believe her own stupidity at trying to cut corners for a change. Everything she'd done so far had been meticulously planned, but that crippled detective and her sidekick were getting a whole lot closer, and that was something that was really starting to spook her a bit.

When she'd launched herself from the steel hull of the narrowboat and swum to the other side of the canal, Jenny had struggled with the restrictions of being fully clothed. She'd also managed to catch one of the pockets of the old army jacket she'd nicked from a second-hand shop a few years back on one of the hooks on a hatch door when fleeing. That was another thing that annoyed her, although she hadn't had a chance to stop and think it through properly at the time.

As soon as she'd reached the far bank, Jenny had clambered up onto the muddy path and headed straight into the trees, despite being soaked from head to foot. Regretting it now, she'd stripped off the jacket, dumped it in the bushes and believed she'd hidden it well enough before setting off towards the street. She'd been very tempted to step inside a riverside pub she'd walked past in order to use the toilet and see if they had one of those decent hand dryers that would be powerful enough to allow her to dry out some of her clothing. On that occasion, common sense had taken control and told her to avoid attracting any unwanted attention to herself. Most of those places had CCTV cameras installed nowadays and she really couldn't afford to be caught on one of those bloody things. That was another reason she always tried her best to stick to the side roads rather than any of the main ones.

The whole world was becoming more big-brother-like, and it was moving closer and closer to artificial intelligence taking control of everything. Apparently, from something she'd read somewhere just recently, the speed with which AI's would be able to learn would just get faster and faster before spreading like a plague at a rate that humans would be completely unable to stop. It would be just like Pandora's Box being opened then unleashing death and a whole host of unnecessary evils out into the wide world.

Right now, the sooner she got back to the house the better. Tom would be out and hopefully the place would be nice and empty, which would then allow her to get herself sorted out and feel a bit better. She really needed to get her head back on track. She'd have a hot shower, put some dry clothes on and then set about dealing with the stuff she'd been wearing afterwards.

'Damn those fucking cops.' She shouted to no one but herself. 'Why don't they just bugger off and go stick their noses into someone else's business.'

Just as she was cursing, Jenny balled her right hand into a tight fist and never even flinched as her long, sharp fingernails pierced the outer layers of skin on her palm and drew blood. She was certainly a prime candidate for anger management classes. It was either that or serve time on what people once referred to as 'The Funny Farm' many moons ago. That was before everything became so politically correct of course.

*

Rob loved the slowness of the canal and the whole lifestyle that was so far removed from the time he'd served in the armed forces. Yet that attempt on his life had taken him back to a certain place in time for a while. As he pondered about his visit from Liberty and Helen, who he really admired as they were also serving the public's interest, he had a nagging feeling that he should be doing a bit more to help. Sitting moored up back at the same spot where the attack had happened, Rob gazed over at the bank on the far side where he'd watched the figure pull itself from the water before disappearing into the thick density of trees at the back.

A woman passing by as she walked her large lump of a dog, which looked as if it had a larger than life appetite, smiled over at him and gave him a friendly wave. It was no different than most people, seeing as it was part of the etiquette of life down by the waterside. In a moment of inspiration, Rob suddenly had an idea that he felt may very well work to satisfy his imagination.

Grabbing up his keys with the cork float attached; which was necessary in case you ever lost them overboard, he quickly made his way over to the control panel. Starting the engine and letting it idle for a moment or two, while he unhooked the ropes at both the front and the back of the boat, he checked to see if he had a clear path both ways, and then calmly steered the boat over to the far bank before tying it up once again.

Shutting the engine off and locking the doors to avoid any unwanted guests, he then stepped out onto the bank, having done this so many times that he'd lost count years ago; although one of the good things was it never caused him any problems with his leg.

Unaware that Liberty had had limited success with the chances of the forensics team paying a visit to the scene, Rob made his way to the exact same location he'd seen his attacker exit.

Once inside the tree-line, surveillance skills from his army training kicked straight in as he edged slowly forward, scanning every inch of ground spread out before him. He'd only been walking for approximately five minutes when he caught sight of the street up ahead, which just happened to be part of a busy through road from the local village. Rob knew there was a pub close by as he'd eaten there on a few occasions in the past. Just then, the smell of fresh food passed by his nostrils and gave him an instant craving to treat himself to one of their home cooked burgers. Their chunky chips and a nice refreshing pint of lager would go down well, he thought, before spotting something out of the corner of his eye, then shooting off the path to investigate further.

He knew the camouflaged jacket would be the same one his attacker had been wearing, and that was easily confirmed once he moved closer and spotted that the pocket had been ripped off. It was the exact same one that had caught on his door and been taken away as evidence.

Wasting no time, he phoned the number that Liberty had left him and then told her exactly what he'd found once she finally answered. Confirming he'd left it undisturbed but had seen the tear where the pocket had gone missing, he told her he'd be in the pub if they needed to speak to him within the next hour. Liberty indicated she'd get back to him within the next five minutes, so with a huge grin spread across his face; the ex-soldier made his way up to the road and crossed over to the pub to celebrate what he saw as his good deed for the day.

CHAPTER 13

The drive to the house in Chessington didn't take too long, although it hadn't exactly been without incident. There'd been some youngster in a flash car, done up to look a lot sportier that it probably was, and he'd felt he had some sort of jurisdiction on the road that allowed him to drive up the inside lane. It was one that he should legally have turned left from prior to approaching the roundabout, but in his world he obviously felt it perfectly acceptable to leave it to the very last moment before pulling over to the right and cut in front of the car that was just about to cross and go straight ahead. Unfortunately, that car just happened to be Liberty's, and although she was forced to suddenly apply the brakes to avoid an accident, she certainly let her horn tell him she wasn't best pleased about his stupid manoeuvre. What pissed her off more however was the fact that he'd then had the cheek to respond with a very rude gesture of his middle finger before moving ahead.

'That's what I call a 'Seagull'. Helen added, before going on to explain they tended to dive in and cause chaos at times. Liberty laughed at that, despite her annoyance.

They only managed to move a few hundred yards before the traffic finally came to a complete standstill. It was rush hour but the queue was also due to the fact that there was a busy industrial estate just off to the left-hand side with some large lorries trying to get in and out. While they sat and waited, Helen unexpectedly undid her seat belt and got out of the car. She rushed ahead until she reached the car with the twat of a wannabe boy racer in, before flashing her police badge at him.

Liberty watched Helen reading him the riot act and wondered if that would make him change his ways and enable him to be more considerate to other drivers in the future. She already knew what the answer would be, and as soon as Helen returned they discussed what she'd said and both agreed it would probably make no difference whatsoever.

Once they'd finally arrived, Mike answered the door and happily led them into the sitting room before offering them drinks with both women turning down the offer, as they'd already discussed going for a coffee at Jean's Café straight after.

'Listen. We'll be as quick as we can.' Liberty stated, as they started discussing the reason for the visit and asking Mike how things had been since Malik's death.

'I wonder if you can just run that bit past us again Mike.' Liberty asked.

She seemed a little on edge for some reason, which wasn't a great surprise as she'd been lying awake thinking about the case for half the night. She felt quite tired and was still wound up about what that prat had done on the way there.

Liberty quite liked Mike as a person, based on the knowledge she had on him up until now, and helped by the welcome he'd given them when they'd arrived. He was certainly very approachable and certainly gave off some nice vibes. It was a shame the same couldn't be said for the countless number of people she'd interviewed over the years. They sat and listened with great interest when Mike confirmed Jenny had come home in wet clothing a few days ago. Apparently, she hadn't noticed him in the house and had no idea he'd spotted her coming in and acting so strangely.

*

Ten minutes after Mike had given them exactly the sort of thing they'd been hoping to hear, neither of them had even dared believe it would be delivered. The two women left and started to make their way towards the large black VW that Liberty had parked up on the main road rather than the drive. With Helen pushing the wheelchair up the steep hill, they chatted away and tried their best to retain their composure. They'd both agreed that Rob Winter had been a little bit naughty in searching the other side of the canal on his own accord, but the fact he'd discovered the hidden jacket and told them straightaway, sort of let him off the hook as far as they were concerned, especially as everything was finally starting to fall into place.

Moments later, just as they approached the parked vehicle, both women were taken by complete surprise as they spotted Jenny walking towards them striding arm in arm with her boyfriend Tom.

They sensed her brief flash of discomfort as she suddenly spotted them, but that was covered up in an instant as she attempted to act all innocent. Waiting for the couple to draw level with them, Liberty manoeuvred her wheelchair so she could talk directly to Jenny, clarify they'd just had a chat with Mike and ask her to explain why she'd come home all wet last Thursday evening. An odd moment of silence descended then everything seemed to erupt into a scene from a slowed down movie as pandemonium set in.

Jenny completely panicked, shoved Tom into the two of them and then started running down the hill. Liberty had already been expecting something of the sort, and having kept her wits about her; she launched herself forward and gave chase without even thinking about the consequences of her actions.

Jenny was starting to get away as she headed off in the distance, having already gained a head start. Helen felt the gap was already too great, but Liberty had taken a crazy gamble and Helen just stood helpless beside Tom watching in horror as her boss shot downhill in her wheelchair. Somehow she managed to make up the lost ground and it wasn't long before she ended up smashing into the running figure. This brought them both down and despite it being a very unbefitting way for an officer of the law to behave; at least it had given them a result.

Even though that was the incident where 'The Ironside Express' nickname actually started, both women had been physically injured with Helen having already called it in on her phone as soon as she and Tom had started heading towards the scene.

On arrival they found Jenny was out cold, having banged her head against the side of one of the houses she'd been passing before being taken out. Liberty on the other hand was fully conscious, but she had been parted from the wheelchair that lay upturned close by, yet looked undamaged at a glance, which was better than could be said for her.

*

As expected, the team were absolutely buzzing as soon as they heard the news. The call had come in from Helen just over three quarters of an hour ago and the cheer that went up was almost deafening when it happened. Apparently, another car was bringing Jenny Manson to the station to be interviewed, but she was taking Liberty to the hospital to get her checked out following her crazy escapade in the wheelchair, which was briefly explained with an added witticism about 'The Ironside Express'.

Cheryl wheeled back in her swivel chair and ran her fingers through her hair, whilst taking a big, deep breath in the process. She felt thoroughly elated right at that moment and knew her instincts had been spot on. Regardless of the pressures and politics she knew came down from above, with Heather and Liberty always doing their best to keep it away from the rest of the team, everyone was more than pleased with the outcome. So much hard work and endless late nights had gone into it. Cheryl mingled in with all that was going on and passed on her own congratulations before moving back to her desk and feeling sad that Luke hadn't been around and been able to celebrate with them. There would definitely be some kind of piss-up down the pub. There always was whenever a case like this had reached this stage. Just as she was about to open up one of the emails from her inbox on the screen, Cheryl received a gentle tap on the shoulder. Turning, she was more than surprised to find Heather standing over her smiling.

'I've just heard that Liberty's been given the all clear, so she and Helen should be here within the next twenty minutes.' Sitting there unsure about how she should reply, this was soon sorted as Heather continued on.

'Therefore, I'd like you to come down and watch the proceeding along with me if you don't mind. You did really well Cheryl. You're a bright young woman who's demonstrated you have what it takes in a job like this. I personally feel you have a long bright future ahead of you.'

To say she was breath taken would have been a complete understatement, but Cheryl was more than happy to walk from the room with Heather and go downstairs.

*

A quick trip to the local hospital had been required in order to check out Liberty's injuries, but thankfully an X-Ray of her left arm revealed nothing had been broken and all she'd suffered was a sprain that needed some TLC and a decent bit of rest. The open cuts to her knees had been cleaned up and dressed, and apart from another one on the bottom of her chin, which was also sorted out with a large unflattering plaster, she was allowed to leave along with the loan of one of the hospital wheelchairs once the paperwork was completed.

'As if I was going to nick one of theirs?' She'd scoffed

at Helen as she'd added her signature.

One of the wheels on hers had buckled slightly and therefore a temporary one would prove more than useful right now, especially as they still had so much to do between them.

With Helen driving, despite Liberty's endless protests that she was fine throughout the whole journey, the two women finally arrived back at the car park housed at the back of the police station which was very busy with its usual hive of activity. The whole area was fairly large in size with an old portacabin pressed up against the far wall, although this was known to be very damp inside with rumours about some big hairy spiders having taken up residence after being abandoned.

The portacabin had served as an overflow office many years ago, but it really needed to go, as it no longer served any purpose. The yard, as if demonstrating how busy it could be, was chock full of police cars with a few already parked head-on and looking as if they were confronting each other and ready for battle. Fortunately, the vehicles that were needed in a hurry were still left clear at the front as certain protocols existed in all stations alike, so woe betide anyone who elected to flout those unwritten rules, especially where a delay could lead to a possible loss of life.

Before they got out of the car, Liberty could see that Helen was deep in thought and decided to ask what she was thinking.

'That woman really must be badly broken in one way or another. She's not quite right in the head and I'll bet it was more than likely something to do with her childhood. She seems to be a very mixed up individual who needs to dish out her own form of justice, although

I honestly believe the revenge is more for others rather than her. From what I can make out so far, this could also be her way of righting something that went on long before, something that she either had to watch or take part in without having any choice in the matter. I don't doubt that if she'd gained some sort of assistance much earlier on, then none of these deaths would have happened. I reckon Jenny was probably a loner who never sought help at the time and is one of those poor lost souls who just got misplaced somewhere in the system before ending up having to fend for herself.'

'Wow! Where on earth did that lot come from?' Liberty asked with both eyebrows raised to the limit.

'You almost sound as if you feel sorry for her.' There was a distinct moment of silence before Liberty added her words of wisdom.

'Listen, the actions of someone capable of murdering more than one fellow human being suggests that they're damaged goods with internal problems chock full of mechanisms such as anger, hostility and possible isolation issues along with a lack of emotional understanding. Most killers are either born with the evil lodged somewhere deep inside them or it's something that's manifested itself and then developed enough over the years until it finally eats away at every sense of logic and becomes just as bad on the outside.' She paused for breath before going on.

'It dulls any reasonable judgement they may have held previously, and each killing would be seen as being fully justified in its own right with some senseless form of compulsion driving them on so they continue on their crazy path of thoughtlessness. Even when they're finally tracked down and captured, most serial killers deny any suggestion of wrongdoing. They fail to realise the error of their ways right up to the end because there's no such thing as right or wrong in their eyes. Anyone who gets in their way is simply seen as an interference that will be dealt with once they decide the time is right. I can tell you that from experience Hel's, and I for one, definitely wouldn't feel very sorry for them. Added to that, if it wasn't for Jenny, Mark would still be alive.'

That last remark really hit home and within a matter of minutes, Helen's mind was soon fully back on track. The wisdom of Liberty Rock had been spoken and understood.

*

Once inside the police station, with Liberty taking on a couple of remarks about her recently acquired facial decoration, they caught the lift to the basement and found their murderer sitting in the interrogation room, cuffed and waiting for them with a bandage on her head. Jenny had been treated for nothing more than a cut to the back of her head with no sign of concussion. Liberty was more than pleased to hear that news, as that was something she'd been worried about, and known that something as simple as that could have caused all sorts of delays.

With the recording started and knowing Heather and Cheryl were viewing proceedings from the other side of the one-way glass, Liberty and Helen began the usual opening lines before moving on to the more serious stuff. Jenny Manson had already realised her reign of terror was finally at an end, but that still didn't stop her from flashing a strangely troubled smile, which didn't exactly go amiss from Liberty.

Having already glanced around to assess if there was any way of escaping and seeing nothing whatsoever, Jenny just sat and faced the two women with a look of resignation etched right across her face. With the attractive mixed-race one standing before her and the one who was obviously her boss doing most of the talking from where she sat in her wheelchair with a stupid looking plaster on her chin, Jenny knew there'd be others watching and listening to the proceedings.

She'd refused any legal help despite being told it would be in her best interest to have someone representing her, but right now she really didn't give a fuck or want to deal with some jumped up twat in a suit. They'd caught her, she'd done what she had, and now she'd face the consequences which she'd be more than happy to deal with, one step at a time.

'Why?' Liberty asked the young woman sitting before her, who really didn't look anything like the majority of killers she'd had to deal with in the past.

They all studied the young woman very closely as she seemed to open up and start to run over some of the details from her past. They could tell it was both stressful and painful in many ways, and probably something she'd either locked away and hadn't thought about for a long, long time, or most likely it was some sort of memory that plagued her more often than not. This was something Liberty knew about only too well, ever since her shooting way back when?

'When I was a young girl, my parents were murdered in a car crash when some maniac forced us off the road. My father died instantly from the impact with the tree we hit, but I was thrown clear and then forced to watch my mother burn as she screamed in agony whilst trapped inside.' There was an unsettling moment of silence while Jenny just sat staring straight ahead. The woman's mind was obviously fully engaged with that memory from the past as she set about reliving exactly what had happened.

'The bastard who'd caused the crash then returned to see how his handiwork was getting on and literally pissed all over me before he started the fire that killed my mother that day. He looked down at me and reckoned he was giving me a second chance in life. He explained how we all live in a fucked-up world with no need to play by the rules any longer. He told me life was far too short and we were all free to do whatever we wanted to do. He said I'd find out for myself one day, and that's exactly what's happened.' Both women listened intently and could almost feel her pain as she held her head high, stared into space and simply carried on with her explanation.

'I survived. I managed pretty much on my own with what he'd said still haunting me every single night until it finally made some sort of sense. I tried to go straight and managed to get a job to see me through at first, but then some jumped up prick of a manager joined the company and made life hell again. That wanker had some sort of hidden agenda and forced me and a few others out, but it was all so he could look good and make out he was saving money for the company somehow.' Jenny stopped for a moment, let out a big sigh and then continued.

'The next job was crap, but the one after that was really enjoyable until another arsehole joined and did exactly the same sort of thing. What sort of pleasure do those dickheads get from doing things like that?' Liberty and Helen both felt a little uneasy at that point, wondering what they'd have done under the same circumstances.

However, the fact that Jenny had gone on and killed people wasn't any better, and from what she'd told them so far, it certainly wasn't an excuse for doing so. Their main job was to uphold the law and not to make judgements where killings had taken place. A moment of deathly silence followed, and then Jenny clearly began to grow more agitated as the memories started to take their toll and she stared at the floor.

'Don't even try to understand what went on, because you won't. I can tell.' Jenny looked like she'd come to a halt but then carried on and became far more animated despite keeping her head bowed down.

'When Mike started telling me about some of those awful characters he kept coming across on his audits, everything just seemed to fall into place and give me some sort of purpose for a change. I knew I'd finally realised what that freak who'd killed my parents was going on about. That was the moment I decided to take things into my own hands and do what I felt needed to be done.' At that point, Jenny lifted her head and stared deep into the eyes of both the women still sitting across from her. It really wasn't the nicest of feelings, and Liberty knew Helen would be feeling just as she did.

'To be totally straightforward with you, I don't regret a single thing. Essentially, I feel quite pleased that I've helped cleanse the world of some of the shit that's preyed on others who delight so much in causing misery wherever they feel fit.' Helen was the first off the mark, having listened to this killer's speech and knowing she needed to say something just to maintain her own sanity just then.

'If you'd even bothered to listen to what you've just

told us, you'd realise you're actually no better than they were when they were alive. So, don't bother giving us any of that 'holier than thou' crap. You my dear, you're a loser who's about to go down for a long, long time. I can guarantee you'll have plenty of time to contemplate everything you've just told us.'

Liberty knew her partner had been fuming deep inside and trying her best to hold it all back, so she wasn't too shocked by the sudden outburst. She fully understood where Helen was coming from, especially as Mark would still be alive if Jenny hadn't done what she seemed to be so proud about.

What came next was pretty brutal however, as Jenny really lost it.

'Loser, oh no, I'm not a loser. You may wish to rethink that stupid notion you have etched in your stupid copper's head. I'm more than happy to confirm that bastard who murdered my parents changed my life that day. Yet in some bizarre way, he also opened up my eyes to a whole new world of possibilities. He freed me to think outside those restrictions that create the boundaries that get inflicted upon us from an early age then stick with us as we grow up in this crazy existence, we all seem to hold so dear. Everyone becomes far too scared to step outside the lines and we're all expected to stick to the rules and become automatons that serve society and ask how high we should jump when orders are given. You two as policewomen are prime examples of exactly what I'm talking about. And *you*!' Jenny screamed out loud, pointing directly at Liberty. 'You joined the system thinking you were going to make a big difference in making the world a much better place. Yet look at the thanks you've got. Have a good look girlfriend. You're stuck there in that stupid bloody wheelchair and I doubt you even got so much as a thank you for your effort. Well I hope you're well and truly pleased with the life you're leading right now, because I certainly realised in time.'

Both women were a little bit taken aback at the whole accusation and the venomous cruelty with which it had been delivered. In one way, it had come across as a personal attack on Liberty, yet taken into context it was clearly aimed at the whole of society and really helped explain why Jenny's mind had been so totally fucked up from such an early age.

CHAPTER 14

The DNA analysis on the camouflaged jacket had taken slightly longer than expected. Now the results had been checked and approved through the system that would enable them to stand up in court when the time came.

 The initial tests had been carried out with a test using UV light. The highly concentrated intensity allowed the forensics team to identify a whole range of bodily fluids such as blood, sweat, saliva, urine or semen. This could be taken from all sorts of human secretions swabbed from sections of the body such as the nose, mouth, armpits or sexual organs if needed. Items of clothing, such as in this case, were also able to be tested, although further tests would also need to be carried out. The reason for this was other liquids of non-person origin such as glue, juice drinks, gel and toothpaste tended to show up, but these could then cause all sorts of confusion if not handled appropriately.

 Consequently, these would need to be eliminated from the entire process, which always added extra time to the whole shebang. Yet some things needed to be done correctly to avoid the evidence being thrown out of court with the suspect getting off on such technicalities and then being allowed to walk the streets and be able to kill again. That had happened far too many times in the past and made a complete farce of all the time and energy spent on bringing a case to court and seeking justice for the wrongdoings in the first place.

As expected, everything in the legal system was so wrapped up in red tape with the correct protocols always having to be followed along with a whole pile of legislative guidelines in order to maintain the correct balance.

Now they finally had Jenny banged up inside and the good news was the results of these tests had been confirmed as matching her DNA. Liberty was sure this provided enough solid evidence for her to get a result, alongside the recordings of interviews they'd carried out with the woman.

*

Mike Britton wasn't exactly having what he'd normally refer to as one of his better days. Malik was dead, Jenny was now under lock and key awaiting trial for a shedload of murders, and Tom had decided to move out after a massive bust up between them.

It had all happened so quickly and was quite unexpected when it did.

He'd simply sat down with a fresh cup of tea to watch the TV once the two women detectives had left as part of his original plan to catch up on the latest episode of 'Agents of Shield' recorded on the little black box sitting on the bottom shelf under the TV, when Tom had burst in and demanded to know why he'd told them about Jenny coming home soaking wet.

'You lousy, rotten bastard.' He'd screamed.

'They've taken her away and say she's killed all sorts of people, including Malik and one of the cop's boyfriends. They'll lock her up and throw away the key just because you couldn't keep your poxy mouth shut.' Then, and without any warning, Tom had lashed out and thumped Mike straight in the face. It'd been a perfect punch that had sent him flying backwards while Tom simply marched from the room shouting that he could no longer live under the same roof as a grass.

That was why Mike now stood in the bathroom assessing the damage in the mirror. He had a small open cut to the top of his nose and could already tell he'd have a nice shiny black eye on his right side. It was already looking quite swollen and he just hoped the left one didn't follow suit, as he used a flannel to dab at his wounds with cold water.

He was still in the locked bathroom five minutes later when there came a loud bang on the door. He heard Tom shout out a final farewell before the front door was slammed shut rather heavily with Mike knowing he'd be gone for good.

'Enjoy life on your own, you miserable fucking snitch.' That had been the parting message, and one that would resonate in Mike's head for a good long while.

He'd only done what he felt was right at the time, but now his sense of reasoning was asking all sorts of questions that he had no idea about how to answer.

As Tom had quite rightly pointed out, another issue he'd have would be living in a house with no flatmates to talk to. Mike knew he'd be wise to get onto the landlord to try and work out something pretty quick. His ultimate dream would be to share the place with a load of pretty women, preferably Swedish ones that cared very little about walking around the house half naked.

His life may seem shit right now, but there was certainly nothing wrong with dreaming about living up to one's expectations.

*

Tom stopped for a moment and looked around at the underpass in more detail. It was a prime place for a mugger to spring out and attack someone, although he did recall there'd been a rumour of some sort doing the rounds about a young schoolgirl having been brutally murdered by a set of twins, she'd been at the same school with a few years back. There were other stories that some form of bullying had been involved, but that was a bizarre story that must have been hushed up in some way or another, especially as there'd been a spate of other incidents that were all just as strange and having happened around about the same time.

Now the place was a no more than a home for tagging with the locals spraying the walls in the evenings once it grew dark enough. This was around the same time the late-night drinkers vacated the bars along Tolworth Broadway then puked up whatever cheap crap they'd been drinking, which reeked even worse in the mornings when the poor commuters had to pass by. It certainly wasn't the greatest start to the day, by any means.

Tom continued to march on. He was absolutely fuming inside, yet he knew that despite his love for Jenny, she probably *was* as guilty as hell. She'd always hidden things from him and now he'd no doubt find out from the media, exactly what that was all about. Jenny could basically go fuck herself as far as he was concerned right now. In reality, she'd already managed to do that already, but now he just wanted to distance himself from everything around him and start looking after number one for a change.

With the busy traffic on the A3 whizzing past him exceedingly noisily on the other side of the barrier, Tom had no idea what he was going to do once he'd walked past the bowling alley and started heading in the general direction of Chessington. He did have a younger sister called Ruth who lived up that way somewhere. She was currently single and had two kids who he didn't really know too well. They'd never really been what you'd class as close, but he did know which road it was and just hoped he'd recognise the house once he got there. Tom had no idea what number it was but felt sure his sis would be happy to give him a bed for a night or two. Who knows, maybe it was even time to make amends and get to know her and the kids a little bit more. He was their uncle in spite of everything.

*

Jenny had woken up screaming with one of the officers having entered the holding cell to check on her. She'd been having the same dream that had haunted her so often in the past, yet in this instance the tables had been turned, as she was suddenly the one who sat trapped inside the vehicle with the flames devouring her. Even the smell of burning flesh seemed to assault her nostrils as her roasting skin started to blacken and crackle while a young girl stood outside and looked on helplessly through the car window with tears streaming down her cheeks.

Once the officer was satisfied the prisoner had been having nothing more than a bad dream, the metal door to the cell was slammed shut and locked securely from the outside just as it was meant to be. The sound of his footsteps could be heard fading away in the corridor outside and the sense of loneliness really began to hit home. The inside of the cell hadn't exactly been built for comfort. It was incredibly dreary with dull painted walls and included a very uncomfortable bench that was about as basic as you could possibly get.

Jenny Manson no longer gave a damn about what was going to happen next. She just sat staring down with her feet spread apart on the concrete floor without a single sign of emotion showing on her face. The imprisoned woman stared at the blank walls as her thoughts shot back to memories of her victims. In her anguished, nasty little mind, she retained a great deal of affection for what she'd done. She classified it as having achieved something that society would always find repulsive; it was also one thing that most people in their right mind would never even think about doing. It boiled down to the day that maniac who'd killed her parents had turned her life on its head and messed with her brain. She treasured the thought of getting even with nasty, pathetic people who felt they had a right to physically or mentally abuse others and think they could get away with it. Yet what she'd been doing was all very one-way, with the emotional distress of the victims loved ones not even entering her way of thinking. Jenny Manson had become unbelievably cold hearted and totally devoid of any emotional thought or feeling since the death of her parents.

Now she just lay back on the bench waiting for

whatever the future might have in store for her. Jenny believed she was mentally ready for whatever would follow and wasn't even planning anything, although there were still a few surprises yet to come.

*

Liberty must have dropped off at some time during the programme she'd obviously been so engrossed in during the night. She'd lain awkwardly across the sofa and her neck and shoulders now ached with a pain and stiffness that would most likely continue to linger around for a good while yet. The TV was still on with some really fit looking people on one of the shopping channels rambling on about how you could also achieve a six-pack for your abdominals within a remarkably short space of time, once you signed up to whatever it was that they were trying to flog. Then she wondered how long in reality it had taken them to look like they had on the screen. The whole thing was no doubt some big marketing scam, yet the public would still fall for it and buy some of that crap.

Going through the tiresome rigmarole of getting into the wheelchair she was still using from the hospital with a promise of hers being ready before the end of the week, and with daylight breaking through the gaps in her curtains, Liberty slowly worked her way into the bathroom.

Having stripped off her clothing and eased herself across to the toilet, she now appreciated how much easier it was with hers having been adapted as it had. Ending up in the state she was in had been a real eye opener. Spending a penny when she was out was always something of a hardship in most cases. The one at work wasn't so bad, but one realisation was that some places claiming to have a disabled toilet really needed to get their act together. *One step at a time,* she thought, but then realised the irony in what that meant.

Having finished a shower in which she'd concentrated the hot jets of water onto her neck and shoulders for a while, Liberty had checked how the cuts to her knees were coming along before eventually getting dressed and having breakfast. She'd been thinking about Jenny Manson and how that incident so early in her childhood had really screwed her mind and life up. The nutter who'd killed her parents and then pissed all over her sounded completely off his head, and she couldn't help but wonder where he was right now or what he'd gone on and done since. There wasn't much chance of ever tracking him down because it had all been so long ago, plus he could be anywhere in the world for all she knew. There was no doubting that someone like him would have gone on and killed again, but likewise, he could already be banged up in a cell somewhere or be long since dead and buried. That was something she'd ever never know, so there was no point in worrying about it any further.

On the positive side, and getting back to more current events, Jenny Manson's trail was looking to be pretty straightforward. They had more than enough evidence for the conviction to stick, plus she'd already fully confessed on tape, which was something her defence lawyer had really kicked up a big fuss about, once Jenny had given up to the pressure and finally got hold of one to represent her.

Checking she had everything she needed for the long day ahead, Liberty carried out a few final checks and then finally set off. Within a matter of minutes, she'd soon become part of the crazy rush hour traffic moving at a snail's pace towards Kingston's town centre.

*

Everything seemed to just come and go with the whole hideous event finally ending in just under a week. Jenny Manson's trail had come and gone with no great surprises. She'd eventually been sentenced for her reign of crime with a life sentence that carried a minimum of thirty years with the chance of parole not standing a hope in hell for now. Liberty's team had been more than pleased that another danger to society was finally off the streets. The media pressure had finally subsided at long last, and they were now free to get back to doing their day jobs and work on some of their other cases.

*

Life in prison was something that suited some people but certainly not others. All in all, Jenny had settled in quite well and managed to stand up for herself when she'd first been placed inside. Fortunately for her, her cellmate had been well institutionalised over the last six years, and therefore her experience proved invaluable, especially with regard to all the tips on how to survive the first few months. There were some extremely unpleasant initiations that all newbies had to go through in order to be accepted, or rejected, as the case proved to be in certain rather unmentionable cases. Although much of what happened wasn't exactly all that pleasant at the time, Jenny was forced to grin and bear it despite wanting to fight back on many occasions.

She'd sat and listened to all the advice she'd received and fully understood what she needed to do in order to survive. This included vital information on how to avoid being picked on and becoming one of the bullies' playmates, which only continued until they grew bored, although that didn't mean those chosen were completely off the hook. You could see it in their eyes and imagine they were never really at rest ever again, after having been so badly abused.

Doing her best to keep her head down and blending in with whatever and whoever she needed to do so in order to continue on without any real incidents, Jenny was soon seen as one of the regular gang members on her block. From that moment on, life seemed pretty boring and painfully repetitive most days.

Fortunately, time moved on with a great many ideas for leaving the place entering her head and being played around with, to see if they'd be possibilities at some time in the future. Other things that came to mind were certain paybacks for people who'd let her down on the outside. For some strange reason the face of that pompous looking woman who'd peered down her nose at her and been part of the jury on the day she'd been sent down, was looking to be quite high up on her list of possible choices.

The longer Jenny was imprisoned and allowed to get her head around the way the system worked, the more some of the potential opportunities looked like they may well have a decent chance of working. Then, as time continued to pass by, a bit more planning gradually took place along with some regard to a few of the finer details that would no doubt be needed at a later date.

CHAPTER 15

'Cheers.' They shouted, as they clunked their wine glasses together with Liberty smiling across at her partner. She was pleased they shared the same sort of interests and were happy enough to discuss work, even though it was way past working hours and they should really have been relaxing. Thinking about that subject alone was not really worth going into any further. Cops working hours didn't necessarily follow a pattern that made any sort of sense. Just like doctors and nurses and other occupations of a similar ilk.

The rest of the team were busy celebrating in the background and even Heather had managed to make a brief appearance at the pub to buy a round of drinks for them all before making her apologies and having to shoot off to a pre-arranged engagement. They could be a right noisy bunch at times, and they certainly had every reason to be joyous after such a long hard case.

Regrettably, there was a profound sense of sadness still hanging over the team as Luke King should certainly have been sitting there amongst them right now. Sadly, the sight of Cheryl Burgess also acted as an additional reminder whenever she appeared, despite what happened to Luke being nothing to do with anything she'd done. In actual fact, the woman had done them all very proud and would bring much more to the team moving forward. The trick was to keep hold of her for now, as word about someone like her soon worked its way around the police grapevine. A bright young cop who had a special knack of spotting things early was always a big bonus to the force, and those with enough clout to do so would always push the boundaries to ensure they got what they needed, by only having the best.

 As they sat and talked work, hoping no one else from the team was listening in, they discussed a couple of open cases they'd been working on. Unfortunately, these had taken a bit of a backseat until the Manson case had finally been closed. Liberty was mulling around with a few ideas on one of them, but she still wanted to check out a few more facts before running it by Helen.
 Looking across at her partner and confirming she'd more than earned her respect in the time they'd been working together; Liberty knew that one more drink each would send them both over the top and they'd end up having to get cabs back home. Their cars were safe enough being tucked away in the police station car park, so it was no problem when the two women happily agreed to another drink when Karen Williamson, one of the more serious members of the team who'd been in the job for over six years, made the offer.

*

Since being confined to a wheelchair, Liberty no longer had the appetite for alcohol as she'd had before. The occasional glass of chilled rosé normally went down quite well, but even that was only when she was in the right sort of mood, which tended to be few and far between. For some reason her willpower seemed to have increased, and that had been pretty exceptional in the first place, compared to others she knew. She'd tried her best to forget about it while being with Helen and the team during the celebrations, at least that was until Karen had joined them and stuck her oar in. Having drunk more than she'd hoped however, along with suffering the consequences the next morning, this wasn't made any easier with her disability which only served as an added wake-up call. There was no point it seemed. Life had already dealt her a bitter blow, so what was the purpose of adding to it? Maybe she was just feeling a bit sorry for herself. Then she wondered how Helen had coped. She was sure she'd downed more than she had. Not that she'd been keeping count at all.

*

Tom's sister had initially been a bit shocked to see him roll up unannounced without any notice on her doorstep. But after letting him in and remembering he actually had a good heart and always looked out for her when they were younger, she felt that having a man around the house would probably be a good idea. It could be quite a rough neighbourhood at times, especially for someone who had two young kids to look after. Matthew was seven and Katie was five, going on eighteen.

What Tom hadn't expected however, was another

tenant. Laken was a very pretty young woman with long blond hair and a fantastic figure, who also lived in the place and payed rent, which was undoubtedly kept quiet from the local authorities. The house was a council house, but Tom wasn't all that fussed. It gave him a roof over his head for now, but he did wonder what sort of relationship existed between his sister and this other woman.

The kids proved to be hard work at first, especially once they realised Tom was actually 'Uncle Tom', but it didn't take long before they all started gelling along really well.

Laken reminded Tom of Jenny a little. That was mainly because she liked to walk around scantily dressed and tease him once the kids had finally gone to bed. He tried to keep on his best behaviour because he couldn't afford to be without a roof over his head right now.

Tom had gone along to Kingston Crown Court and witnessed Jenny get sentenced to a long stretch in prison before making the decision to just cut her out of his life altogether. He realised she'd been nothing but trouble from the start, once he eventually sat and reflected on the time he'd spent with her. He sure as hell wasn't about to waste time visiting her and having to go through all the rigmarole that went with gaining entry just for the sake of sitting and chatting about nothing in particular. Who gave a fuck about the weather or what was happening in the world right now? He'd already decided he'd be looking after number one from now on, and that was about to start there and then. Therefore, as far as he was concerned, it was a matter of Goodbye Jenny, you fucking mad bitch. Enjoy your time in the poke and have a good life if they ever decide to set you free one day.

During the court case, Tom had also met up with an old family acquaintance; a lady by the name of Danielle Hinckley-Smith who'd been sitting on the jury. Due to the security involved and the nature of the case, they hadn't really had any time together, but Danielle *had* told him to send her a friend request on Facebook, so they could keep in touch. This wasn't something Tom tended to use that much, but he did have an account, and so he promised to do so before she finally shot off.

'It really was a small world sometimes.' He thought, as he walked down the stairs.

*

Laken had been working hard on Tom for the last few months. Her little seduction games were something that gave her real pleasure and she knew he really had the hots for her. He'd settled in well and didn't seem all that bothered when he'd walked in on them one night, having caught her and his sister in the middle of a sexual engagement. On that occasion Tom had just shot upstairs and gone straight to bed, yet Laken having spotted him, then mentioned it to Ruth who didn't really seem too bothered. It was her place after all, so from her point of view she could do whatever she wanted within those four walls.

One evening, after Tom had promised to look after the kids, with his sister having gone out on a hen night with some of her old schoolmates and planning to be away for the whole night, he found himself sitting together in the living room with Laken. They'd both been drinking a few beers and watching a thriller when it suddenly changed halfway through and became incredibly erotic in places. As the film had gone on, they'd both slouched over and come together on the sofa. Then they'd both gone reasonably quiet and appeared to be a little bit embarrassed about the whole thing for the first few minutes. Yet as soon as Laken turned and looked directly into Tom's eyes, she knew he was feeling incredibly horny, just as she was. She'd also taken a glance down and noticed the bulge in his trousers, which was a bit of a giveaway. Laken scarcely had a chance to say anything before he moved his head forward and his mouth engaged hers. With the forceful touch of their lips coming together so firmly, Laken knew she'd be putty in his hands from that point onwards. The young woman, who'd originally been born in Malta, soon found herself reaching over and placing her hand to the side of his neck before opening her lips to enable his tongue to intermingle with hers.

Despite her initial doubts about what Ruth may have to say about any form of relationship between her and her brother, which both came and went in the same instant, Laken simply decided to just go with the flow and purposely pressed herself even harder against Tom. Laken caught her breath as he swiftly returned the gesture then took her face between his hands with a full understanding of where things would be heading from then on. Both were willing their bodies to join together even further as the waiting game soon came to an abrupt halt and their sexual desires took full control. Without wanting to hang about any longer, Tom pulled apart ever so slightly then reached a hand out for the front of Laken's red sweatshirt. He worked quickly as soon as she lifted her arms up to enable him to ease the whole thing up and over her head. He ran his hands up the smooth, silky sides of the woman's striking body and grew even harder at the thought of where things were about to lead. She wasn't wearing a bra underneath and both breasts swung free as the top slipped to the floor.

It had been quite a while since he'd last had sex, with Jenny now banged up inside. Fortunately for him, Laken couldn't remain all that patient either, as she also hadn't had sex with a man for a while. Now she was desperate to feel him deep inside her and wanted it really bad. With his T-shirt already removed, Laken scrabbled around impatiently with the brass button and the zip on his jeans, but within a moderately short space of time the blue denim had also joined the growing pile on the floor in front of the TV.

The pair of them were soon completely stark naked and lying sprawled across the sofa with Tom's fingers searching out and finding her secretive places. Her juices were well and truly overflowing by that time, and the more he worked to get her aroused, the more she reacted and moaned. Laken gave out a loud but beautiful sounding sigh as Tom continued to ease his fingers in and out of the damp stickiness of her vagina. She couldn't help but place her hand down beside his and feel her own wetness while she pleaded for him to keep going and never ever stop.

The two of them were so caught up in the moment. They moved around and worked incredibly well together until Tom judged he'd almost managed to bring Laken close to the edge of release. While Tom had been working away on her, Laken had been busily teasing his long, hard shaft and now felt his hardness rub up against her as he moved and tried to reposition himself on top of her. As he grabbed at her hips and attempted to work his way around to where he needed to be, Laken eagerly spread her legs apart and helped him place his fully erect penis inside her. She couldn't help but cry out in sheer delight as he entered her with ease. They both worked in complete unison to build up a decent rhythm as Tom urgently thrust his buttocks back and forth while looking deep into this amazing blonde's eye's. He knew she was experiencing the same feelings that he was, and this only served to drive him on. They were soon going at it hammer and tongs and working up a right old sweat between them. With no other option than to let his own needs go first, which caused him to repeatedly drive deeper and deeper inside her. Tom was not to know that Laken would start to climax at exactly the same time. He felt as if all his dreams had come true all of a sudden. It was almost as if they'd been destined to be together from the day they'd been born. Laken felt one last wave of pleasure wash right through her lower body before letting out a small but delicate scream as if to let him know how well he'd done. To say that Tom was on a complete high by that time would have been a massive understatement, but he made sure he rode the woman right to the finish before finally collapsing on top of her exhausted. Both were feeling extremely proud of their efforts as they cuddled up together, shared the warmth of each other's bodies and lay there recovering before deciding to get started on a repeat performance.

*

Serena Mack, having resorted back to her maiden

name, was one of those lucky women gifted with an amazing body that had a metabolism that enabled it to age much slower than any of her friends and family. She'd borne three children into the world during her marriage, but that was when life had seemed to offer just about everything she'd always wished for. Unfortunately, that was before it eventually came crashing down around her shoulders and led her to the life she now lived and breathed every single day. Serena was fair haired, maintained a well-trimmed figure and had a nice pair of long attractive legs that still managed to turn men's heads, especially if she chose to wear the correct gear, depending on the type of mood she happened to be in at the time. She had two boys and a girl who now lived with her ex-husband, following what she felt had been a right royal fuck-up by her legal team in court. They'd now been divorced for well over four years and the whole thing had turned very messy with Peter gaining full custody due to her string of love affairs with numerous lovers being well and truly exposed, much to her embarrassment at the time. As always, it had been the lawyers being the ones who came out winning in the long run.

Her husband, Peter Satterthwaite was a manager in a telecommunications company, having worked his way up through the ranks from an apprentice many moons ago. He'd always been highly ambitious and it was a mixture of hard work and sheer determination that had gotten him to where he was today. Serena had known many of his colleagues as she'd visited his office on a few occasions, plus of course there'd been a whole host of Christmas parties and other such get togethers over the years. She quite liked most of them, but her husband never really had a good word to say about any of them, especially Rowena, who he particularly liked to have a good old moan about for some strange reason.

Peter had first met and fell in love with Serena back in the early eighties, during the days of Duran Duran and the Human League, when the New Romantic Movement was happily rolling along in all its glory. Sadly, time had long moved on and he'd clearly had no idea she was shagging around, whereas everyone around him seemed to have known about it for ages, which naturally made him the laughing stock once all was revealed. The kids were surprisingly resilient to the whole thing for ones who were so young, but in truth he was a good father to them and never complained when Serena requested access to them, despite the fact he could have fought quite easily and won.

To say he was fuming inside was a bit of an understatement as Peter was one of those people who appeared all wonderful and bubbly on the outside but kept his inner thoughts and feelings very much to himself.

CHAPTER 16

Life in prison had become pretty dull after a while. It tended to be very repetitive and mind-numbing, yet things moved on with ideas for leaving the place continuing to head inbound to some of the more innovative and imaginable sections of the prisoners rather unusual mind.

'Well I guess this gives me another period to run riot in, so let's see how I can fix a few things.' Jenny thought to herself as she sat totally bored to tears in her cell. *'Tom will be my first port of call because he actually cares for me, but let's see how prepared those dear cops Liberty Rock and that precious sidekick Helen Morgan are for what they rightfully have coming their way,'* She continued, quaking with delight at the very thought of what she was planning to do, despite the fact it was still work in progress for now. *'That snotty cow who was part of the jury, the one who'd looked down her nose at her as if she'd been something she'd trod in, could also do with a few lessons, but how the hell was she likely to find out who she was?'* That would have to wait, she

guessed, as there were more important things to sort out first. Life did tend to have a funny old way of working things out sometimes, and Jenny certainly had time on her hands right now.

*

Liberty wasn't exactly what she'd class as being in the greatest of moods as she pulled up outside her home and parked within the marked white lines. She gave out an audible sigh before releasing the wheelchair from the lock on the floor which was basically designed to stop her from moving around whilst driving. With the powered tailgate and automatic foldout ramp doing their business in allowing her to leave unaided through the rear of her prized VW Caddy in a more than dignified manner, she wheeled herself away and hit the remote which automatically closed up the back of the car before heading up the ugly ramp that led to her front door.

Once inside, the DCI made herself a cup of tea and tried her best to calm down. Why were so many members of the public so bloody ignorant about people who lived with disabilities? Had she really been that unaware before she'd ended up as she had herself? She certainly didn't think so.

She'd been sitting quite happily looking out over a pond just admiring the wildlife going about their daily business, when a family comprising of a man, his wife, their two young girls and a small yappy dog literally went and stood directly in front of her, completely blocking her view.

A few minutes later the woman had turned and said, 'Oh sorry! Are we standing in your way?' Liberty, who'd already seen red and been doing her best to bite her tongue, just simply replied,

'Oh no! You just carry on. I was just sitting here for the fun of it and admiring the grass.' She recalled how the woman had given her a right funny look before conversing with her husband then moving on with both girls and the dog in tow.

'Good riddance to a bad bunch,' Liberty had muttered quietly to herself, but not feeling any better for doing so. It was the same story on most days, yet something she'd had no choice but to get used too. The worst people were the ones who didn't believe she really needed to be in the wheelchair or badgered her to know what had happened. Yet, those were mostly random strangers who she'd never even clapped eyes on before.

Making a cup of tea and thinking about having another attempt at her knitting, which was sort of working out okay but still needed quite a bit of work on the improvement front, Liberty knew she secretly enjoyed her new-found hobby, despite the fact she was incredibly good at dropping stitches and losing her knitting needles down the side of the sofa.

*

Jenny had noted earlier on when she'd first arrived that one of the guards in the female prison appeared quite similar to her in both looks and stature. Her name was Ramona, or Rambo, as most inmates and guards tended to call her. There'd even been a few odd occasions when others had pointed out the likeness to her.

Fortunately, it turned out Ramona was one of the nicer guards, hence Jenny had already decided to use this to her advantage when she'd been busy plotting her escape and doing her best to keep it secret from everyone else.

When the day finally came, and she felt everything was about as ready as it could be, she'd already made sure Ramona was on duty in her section and her cellmate wasn't still hanging around. She'd put on a great act of sitting in the cell crying and hoping her sobs would be heard by the passing guard. Sure enough, it was Ramona who appeared and gave her the very sympathy she'd been seeking. Fully aware of what needed to be done, Jenny moved fast and managed to overcome the woman by knocking her completely unconscious with two heavy blows to the head. She then gagged her, stripped her of her uniform and placed her face down handcuffed to the bed with a sheet covering her body so it looked like she was sleeping.

Walking away, impersonating Ramona and remaining confident in what she was doing went surprising well. It even lasted right up until she was outside in the grounds, which went far better than she'd ever expected.

The main reason for that would have been the lack of personnel and everyone being so busy with everything being so tightly stretched in the prison service due to the ever-increasing cuts in government funding. Still, that wasn't her problem, and maybe they'd learn a lesson from her escape. Maybe she was actually doing them a favour...

Jenny hadn't felt any remorse about the fact she'd had to use a bit more force on Ramona to shut her up than she'd expected, but at least she hadn't killed her. Now, on the opposite side of that, she felt nothing whatsoever for the sentry in the guardhouse who she'd never set eyes on before. Jenny had to move fast once again and happily used the baton on the unsuspecting victim without mercy. She beat him around the head a few times with a lot more force than she'd probably needed, yet that was only because she really couldn't afford for anything to get screwed up, especially as she'd managed to get so far. The sight of blood pouring from the wounds on the man's head never worried her one iota, although she was very careful not to stand in any of it. Admittedly, there was a lot more than expected. But Jenny simply watched as it began to pool away from the body that now lay across the floor in the small hut which had already more than served its purpose.

Locating the keys to one of the five cars in the outer car park and using it to escape hadn't been that hard either, once she'd eventually found the right vehicle that matched. She was well aware that time had already started running out; and there was more than a good chance that Ramona had already been discovered in her cell, with her escape having finally been rumbled. Jenny drove off along the weathered road that led away from the remote prison site like a bat out of hell. Her mind was now fully focused on the likely tactics her pursuers would be most likely to use, and she certainly had no plans about being caught.

Jenny however, was nobody's fool. She'd used her common sense to ditch the car much earlier than would have been expected and hid it from sight on knowing they'd be searching for that one specifically. She was also well aware she'd be shown no mercy if they managed to catch up with her, not only because of the killing and the attack on Rambo, but also based on the fact she'd managed to outwit them and made them look incompetent.

Although she was still much closer to the prison than she actually wanted to be, Jenny had already decided this ruse was a far better plan and would hopefully give her a bit more time, as every second was crucial. The authorities would be on the lookout for the stolen car and concentrating their efforts on an area much further away according to logic. Doing her best to stay undercover by sticking close to the large abundance of trees and hedges along the narrow country lanes, she also utilised some of the fields that were available, rather than braving the main roads.

Jenny did her best to ensure she could easily get under cover if need be, as she continued to walk on and work out what she'd best do next. Drinking down a huge mouthful of the wonderful fresh air on offer and feeling the soft earth beneath her feet, she listened to all the delightful sounds that nature was throwing in her direction. She was now even more determined not to get caught as her resolution grew stronger.

Another factor was the point she had quite a few things to catch up on once she was finally sorted and things had finally begun to die down.

*

Once free and sensing no one was following directly on her heels, Jenny broke away from the forest clearing whilst keeping her eyes peeled for any unusual signs of movement, both around her and up in the sky. If a helicopter were to be involved in the search, and she was under no illusion that that wouldn't be the case,

Jenny knew she'd have to get back under cover in an instant. After another twenty minutes of walking with nothing to see apart from endless fields and trees for company in such a remote area, she eventually slowed as she spotted what looked to be a roof of some sort. It appeared as if it was attached to a smallish building just over in the far distance.

Changing her direction and bearing further off to the right, Jenny swiftly headed towards it with renewed vigour. Once she'd cleared away from the tree-line to a much more open section of land, she managed to pick up her pace again and smiled at her good fortune. This improved even more once she spotted some clothing hanging out on the washing line and recognised it as belonging to a woman, as she moved ever closer.

Reaching the side of the house and hoping whoever lived there hadn't noticed her approaching, Jenny remained surprisingly patient as she waited and watched to see if there was any sign of movement or any possible clue as to who the occupant could be.

Fortunately, her endurance paid off as a pretty looking woman who she judged to be about the same age as her, suddenly appeared in the back garden dressed in a skimpy dress that was barely there. Then, as the sun caught her at a certain angle, Jenny was more than convinced she was completely naked underneath.

Just that thought alone was enough to awaken a long forgotten sexual interest hidden deep within her body, then without even thinking of the risks involved, Jenny stepped straight out into the open and tried to act all surprised.

'Oh, I'm really sorry to disturb you in your beautiful house. I was hitchhiking across this neck of the woods but I'm afraid I'm a bit lost and in need of a little guidance if you could be so kind.' The woman looked directly into her face, yet despite sensing the stranger wasn't telling the whole truth, Jenny somehow knew she was now in good hands. There was something deep inside the woman's eyes that told her she was a kindred spirit of sorts, and that was the moment the story she'd been told about a person's eyes being a doorway to their soul, suddenly made a whole lot more sense.

Lana Meyer was originally from Holland and had come across to England to escape her lifestyle and create a new one where she could be alone and live the remote existence she'd been craving. Although she was little weary at first, Lana welcomed Jenny into her home and as soon as she heard she didn't need to be anywhere in particular for now, she'd offered her a bed for a few nights then gave her something to eat and drink while they sat and talked.

Although Lana had been living a life of solitude and enjoyed such an existence, now that Jenny had turned up she soon realised she'd wanted the company of another person for quite a while but had been far too afraid to admit it. Jenny had already made it crystal clear she was keen to move on once she'd sorted herself out properly, and therefore, Lana knew she needed to make the most of their short time together.

Maybe Jenny was heaven sent, she wondered inside her head, although Lana wasn't exactly religious in any way. Yet she did strongly believe in fate.

*

Peter Satterthwaite wasn't having what he'd have classed as one of his better days. The whole thing had started with his alarm clock having thrown a wobbly, and then deciding to take a last-minute vacation for some curious reason. This had been followed by him rushing around the house in a crazy panic, screaming at Serena and the kids, then totally losing it when his electric razor only half shaved him because it wasn't fully charged. It didn't help matters any further when the shampoo went in his eyes while he was showering, and the water turned cold halfway through. Yet, after managing to make it into work just a few minutes later than he normally would, along with his added allowance of road rage during the journey being pretty impressive for what one might term; a slightly irritated man, Peter plonked himself down in his black leather chair and let out an incredibly deep sigh. To say his life was not in the best of places right now would have been an understatement. It really didn't help matters when he stared in bewilderment at his desktop and realised he'd been an even bigger idiot than he'd realised by having left his laptop at home, which happened to have just about everything he needed for that day sitting on it. The man, who was already bedraggled and feeling rightly pissed off by that time, simply raised himself up, muttered a few choice words to no one in particular, then kicked his chair before heading back off towards the stairs leading back to the building's car park.

Returning to the office forty-five minutes later in a right stroppy mood, especially as the traffic had been so much worse the second time around, Peter was almost at his wits end when he realised he'd now gone and left his laptop charger at home. Fortunately, this wasn't such a disaster as the lady called Susan who sat just a few desks away and always seemed to have a heart of gold, had managed to come to his rescue and let him share hers as she was already showing 100% charge.

The woman had never seen Peter in such a state before, so was genuinely surprised at his sudden turn of behaviour. What also helped the situation was the fact she also happened to have a bit of a soft spot for him, and had done so for a good many years.

Something pretty serious was obviously troubling the poor man, and that soon set her mind off racing in all sorts of ways. But then she started to wonder if all those rumours she'd heard about his wife could possibly have had a ring of truth about them. It was definitely a possibility, and that alone would certainly go towards explaining what was happening with him right now.

Her colleague, Rowena had told her she'd never really trusted him, but Sue hoped she was seriously wrong in her judgement of the man.

*

Lana really enjoyed her lesbian tendencies and had always wanted to explore them even further if the chance should ever happen to arise, especially before she grew too old and boring to experiment. Therefore, Jenny turning up as she had was almost a gift from heaven. She'd really been starting to get fed up with the limited number of sex toys she had shut away in the bottom drawer of her bedside cabinet. Lana assumed most people went through various stages in their lives where they wanted to try a little bit of everything. From what she'd gathered in the papers and TV, alongside the occasional visit to town or even through a trip to the cinema, it appeared a lot of women were much more liberal and open about sex nowadays. It was also in just about every magazine you looked in, plus it was readily available at the click of a button if you were prepared to sit and search the internet, which was something she preferred to avoid.

Although Lana tended to steer clear of the TV and computer wherever possible, she still had full access along with a live account. Living so remote was fine up to a certain point, but it was almost impossible to let it all go once you'd been using it for so long.

CHAPTER 17

Lana apologised she only had the one bed, but informed Jenny she was more than welcome to crash out on the sofa, even though it wasn't exactly the most comfortable of places to sleep on.

The alternative offering had been to share *her* bed, which was more than big enough for two people. It was a king-size one after all. So that was what Jenny opted for without even giving it a second thought. The night had gone incredibly well with most of the produce coming directly from Lana's garden, although they cheated with the wine, as that was from a supermarket in the next town.

Lana seemed to have everything sussed and was coming across as being very self-sufficient in more ways than one. Having gone upstairs for the night and now sitting together on the end of Lana's bed with its cute little on-suite bathroom, music from one of her favourite groups; The Counting Crows was playing away in the background and adding to the ambience of the night.

As Jenny stood and pulled her top up and over her head in a knowingly seductive way, Lana stared up and gazed longingly at the woman. Feeling incredibly horny and with her head at the same height as Jenny's well-toned stomach, she took a gamble, moved her head forward and planted a kiss directly over her belly button. Jenny smiled as she released the clip on her jeans then quickly unzipped them before allowing them to drop to the floor. She now stood before Lana wearing only the briefest of sexy red silky knickers and simply slipped her hand down the front. Studying Lana's face as she continued to gaze with an obvious desperation that said she wanted to become part of the action, Jenny continued to tease her but couldn't resist pulling the skimpy material slightly aside to expose her womanhood. It clearly begged for attention and the urge to slip her tongue out and put it to work was far too much to bear any longer.

Jenny had wanted it to happen just as much, and she'd now become very wet. She held firm as she gazed down and watched Lana getting to work, using one of her fingers to help create a nice ripe opening as she explored its intoxicating depths.

Naturally, the young Dutch woman was also becoming enormously aroused, as she also felt herself becoming wet down below whilst carrying on and savouring every glorious minute. Jenny let out a couple of gentle sighs just to confirm she was getting incredibly close to the point where she'd be completely unable to hold back any longer. This just spurred Lana on even further as she then upped the speed and increased the pressure of her fingers.

Jenny reached down and pulled off Lana's skimpy dress before grabbing her pert breasts and working her into a wild frenzy. Lana had already managed to slip off the thong she'd been wearing, so they were both completely naked by now. As they positioned themselves more comfortably onto the bed, it wasn't too long before they were fully entangled and pleasuring each other with what looked to be the fervour and wanton craze of a newly married couple.

*

Jenny woke up in a complete frenzy. She'd been suffering the same old dream and watched helplessly as the terrifying flames devoured her mother while she sat trapped inside the car. She immediately kicked the duvet aside and shot straight out of the bed.

Having left Lana's place following a few weeks of working to get herself back together, she'd returned to the remote run-down house she'd originally lived in before meeting Tom. Jenny had given this a lot of thought prior to leaving Lana. She knew she'd still be very safe for now, plus this place was completely off the radar as far as anyone else was concerned.

Apparently, it had belonged to some old lady who'd died with the managing agents just wanting to rent it out cheaply with a promise it would eventually be modernised. She'd used another name at the time, kept herself pretty much to herself, and only visited the local shop when she'd really needed to. Jenny had also taken out a long-term rental agreement, and because she'd paid the whole lot off in advance, the agency had simply washed their hands of the place, especially as it was a complete win, win result for them.

Lana had taken her departure quite badly, but Jenny had made it more than clear that she couldn't afford to become too involved with someone for now.

Having returned, and feeling reasonably safe in the shabby old place, Jenny now stood naked in front of the cracked bathroom mirror with a pair of sharp scissors held in her right hand. She gazed hard at the face staring back at her and hardly recognised herself as the young kid who'd watched her parents die at such an early age and then been left to fend for herself. Bringing the shiny blades up towards her face, she moved the point very close to her right eye for a moment before finally attacking the long locks of black hair. Jenny hacked away at the ends and didn't have a care in the world as the strands glanced off her body, landing in a heap around her bare feet. It took a while, but eventually she was able to look up and admire her handiwork. Short hair with a boyish look was supposed to be all the rage at one time, and Jenny felt the result looked far better than she'd been expecting. She was certain Lana would have loved this new look and approved of it in her own unique way. It would have been quite interesting to have gone out at night and seen what sort of response she would have picked up on her gaydar. Unfortunately, time was of the essence right now, and most likely to fight her all the way.

Having undergone a cold shower, as there was no hot water in the place; Jenny managed to get through then tidy up after herself. She'd carefully placed the hair clippings into a plastic shopping bag, and then planned to dump them in a bin as soon as she passed one out on the street.

Finding the keys exactly where she'd left them, Jenny walked around the back of the house then started up the old car she'd been using before. It was a bit of an old banger, but it had always been reliable and certainly wouldn't draw any unwanted attention to her.

It had been a good call to return to the house to check if the drugs and needles she'd hidden at the back of the cupboard under the stairs would still be there. She hadn't doubted it for a moment, because they'd been well hidden away in a section that was very, very difficult to spot. Jenny knew the police would have carried out a thorough search of the room she'd shared with Tom following her arrest, so the thought of storing things there would never even have entered her mind. It was a major part of her DNA to think ahead and plan for any unexpected circumstances, and that had just paid off, as she now had the tools she needed to continue where she'd left off before being put in the slammer.

There were still a few scores that needed to be settled, and that included a certain DCI and her stunner of a sidekick.

*

Aware of Tom's social media login name and password, and then using a local internet café's PC under a false name with her new look working incredibly well for now, Jenny had already managed to track down Tom as living at his sister's house. Now she'd fully confirmed where he was staying, she felt quite pleased things were starting to fall into place at last, especially as she still had a lot more ground to cover before she'd be satisfied.

One thing she hadn't expected however, was to find the face of the stuck-up cow who'd been sitting all smug-like in the jury staring right back at her from the screen. Jenny worked out from the link on Tom's

Facebook page that her name was Danielle Hinckley-Smith. She had no doubt the bitch had wanted her sentenced and shut away for a good long time, just as she had been, yet that was something Jenny had convinced herself as being the case a while ago. Now a chance at doing something about it had been laid quite plainly in her lap, as if it had been some strange quirk of fate. It had been quite a shock to find her picture among his list of friends, but even stranger to link to her page and find that arrogant looking face staring out at her and willing her to do something nasty. That was what triggered her to recall the words of her parent's murderer from the day her life had completely been transformed.

'I'm giving you a chance kid. It's a big fucked up world we live in right now, so there's no need to play by the rules any longer. Just take what you want and do whatever you wanna do. Don't let people take advantage of you and just make sure you get payback on anyone who pisses you off. Life's too short kid, and that's something you'll eventually find out for yourself someday.'

That was how she remembered those words. They'd become totally engrained in her head from that day onwards. Of course, she'd realised for herself how true they were many years ago, but times like this were proving to be the proper test. Even now, Jenny could feel her adrenaline starting to rise as she dreamed up a whole host of how things could possibly pan out as she sat there thinking of the plan she'd come up with.

A few days later, luck was definitely on her side as she chose another street and played out the same scam with much more success this time around. Jenny had parked up one evening then boldly walked up to a door and knocked twice. She'd been scouring the Thames Ditton area for a while and kept her eyes peeled for any sign of the woman she'd been seeking. She knew she was close as her senses told her so. These were very rarely wrong, and she trusted them immeasurably. Just after a minute or two, an old lady answered the door and asked what she wanted.

'I'd like to speak to Danielle if she's in please, she asked politely.

'I'm sorry to say you have the wrong house young lady. I do know there's a Danielle who lives about four doors down in that direction', she offered, pointing to the left. 'It's the one with the red door and the large drive in front of it. It's much bigger than mine because all those houses were built a lot later than these ones.'

'I'm really sorry to have disturbed you,' Jenny apologised, waving her hand in the air and trying her best to look sincere.

'Thanks so much for your help and I hope you have a good evening,' she shouted, before turning and bounding up the pathway leading back to the street.

Jenny sat a short distance away, so as not to raise any unwanted attention. She watched the house from her car before confirming she'd hit the jackpot when Danielle eventually appeared around the corner pushing a baby in one of those modern-day buggy's. They didn't exactly come cheap, and the whole neighbourhood stank of money. Now she knew exactly where the stupid bitch lived, she just needed to work out a way of delivering payback as a few ideas already began to circle around in her distorted mind.

Jenny waited a while before starting the engine then

drove away with the young mother being totally oblivious to anything that had gone on. The jury service she'd attended had long gone from her mind, plus she was one of the last people on the planet who'd ever make a judgement against another person. The truth of the matter was Danielle Hinckley-Smith was one of the nicest characters you could ever wish to meet. She was well loved by everyone who knew her and had so much to live for, especially with her and her husband being gloriously happy with the journey they were on right now.

*

Jenny sat in the car and waited patiently for the lights to finish their annoying waiting game before turning to green. Why was it you'd have a whole run of green light's when you weren't all that bothered, yet hit a stream of red light's whenever you were in a hurry?

The traffic moved just as she'd been expecting for that time of the day, then a few moments later Jenny reduced her speed and turned left into the side road she'd been seeking, before pulling in to a space and parking up properly.

Disguised with a hat and a pair of crappy sunglasses, whilst knowing that sitting so close to the lion's den was a big risk, Jenny was convinced she'd never be recognised. The woman just bided her time and watched the comings and goings of the police station car park for a while. Hopefully, she'd not have to wait too long, although she did have to be very careful not to get a parking ticket. For now, the area was full of spaces that could only be used for a limited amount of time. Normally the first half hour was free because the local shopkeepers had put up a fight with the local council and won. Yet the chances of being caught going over that time tended to be a bit of a lottery, especially as the wardens drove around on noisy little mopeds and loved to hide out of sight before pouncing at the last moment.

There'd been all sorts of accusations about it being extremely unfair, with the local authority only being interested in making as much money out of drivers as possible. The meters and cameras have proved to be nothing more than cash cows.

There was plenty of movement in and out of the back of the police station, but using her car as cover, Jenny continued to watch and wait. Eventually her patience finally paid off as she watched the dark Caddy pull out with Liberty Rock driving and Helen Morgan sitting alongside her talking about something that made them both smile and appear as if everything in the world was simply wonderful right now.

Following close behind, but without making it obvious they were being tailed, Jenny drove sensibly amongst the current rush of vehicles that all headed in the same direction, before finally separating out and following the Caddy off to the left. Jenny watched as their car indicated and then pulled into a disabled parking space outside a small group of shops. She was forced to stop and wait while a bus eased through, as the road only had a limited amount of space due to a load of cars being parked on her right-hand side. That played into her favour however, as it allowed her to watch Helen get out of the car then wait for her boss's wheelchair to descend from the back.

Turning next right, Jenny also found a parking space before exiting the car and walking back the way she'd just come.

By the end of the day, Jenny had happily achieved exactly what she'd wanted. She now knew the coffee shop they frequented, and this went by the name of Jeans Café. They also came and went from the station quite often, although that would obviously change on a daily basis. Yet more importantly, and literally the best result of the day, was she now knew where both women lived.

It proved to be a fairly long day, and one that had also eaten into the best part of the evening, but at least she'd seen Liberty drop Helen off at home, and then been able to find out exactly where the crippled DCI lived as well. The disabled ramp right outside helped confirm things even further, and she'd even sat and watched the cop struggling to get up and through the front door.

'It couldn't have happened to a nicer woman. You two are certainly on my list of things to do, and I'm really looking forward to renewing our acquaintance ladies.' she muttered to herself before driving off and feeling more than content with her days work.

*

Danielle Hinckley-Smith's eyes showed she was absolutely petrified as she sat securely tied to the chair with her mouth taped up, so she was unable to mutter a word. She was in what seemed to be an old house that was very dark and dismal with the curtains drawn tightly shut. The air was stale, and everything felt horribly damp. The place appeared to be very old-fashioned and looked as if it had stood neglected for a long time and only just started being used again, from what she could gather. It wasn't as if she'd been given the grand tour. All she remembered was attempting to stop on her bike when a young woman stepped into her path at the very last minute and caused her to go flying off onto the grass. Just as she'd been about to get up and protest, something sharp had been jabbed into the side of her neck, and the next thing she remembered was waking up strapped to the chair.

The woman holding her had not spoken so far, so Danielle had absolutely no idea why any of this was happening to her. Her abductor's hair was short and black which made her look almost boyish to some degree, yet her face was actually quite pretty. That was obviously something she didn't want to make the most of, but who was to know what was going on inside her head right now?

As expected, Danielle was already very scared and going half out of her mind. She was trembling all over and having a lot of trouble breathing with her mouth strapped up as it was.

Yet the very fact that this woman had allowed her to see her face was what really frightened her the most. It didn't bode too well according to all those thrillers she'd read and seen on the television. Yet, that was because the victim was always killed in order to stop them identifying the baddie. There was however, something very familiar about the woman's features that she couldn't quite put her finger on right now.

CHAPTER 18

Time had passed remarkably fast. Liberty sat hunched over her desk in her wheelchair ploughing through a stream of emails as she busily placed them in the correct folders laid out in the personal filing system displayed in front of her on the large screen. These included one attempted murder, where the husband had denied any such thing, although a whole stash of evidence was slowly being gathered and not looking as if there'd be much working in his favour. The guy, a manager by the name of Peter Satterthwaite was clearly guilty, but their job was to carry out a full investigation and then make sure the case would stand up in court. They also had three missing persons they needed to investigate a lot further, along with the abduction the team would be about to look into, once Liberty had carried out that morning's briefing.

All in all, it had been coming up to eight months since Jenny Manson had been sentenced   with that having been the last big case they'd worked on. There was always a bit of a lull after the storm, but Helen was also plodding away, sitting one desk along from Liberty and feeling quite irritated. It was the never-ending emails and growing piles of papers involving minor cases that needed to be dealt with correctly, but didn't appear to have much to go on just yet. It was always hard in the earlier stages until you got a proper bite that would set the trail off in the right direction.

Just like Liberty, and no doubt the rest of the team, they all waited in vain for the one notification that would bring the next big case in. It wasn't that any of them wished for someone to be murdered or anything along those lines... It was just what they did. They were a highly regarded team of specialists that needed to be seen busy doing something useful, rather than just pen-pushing.

They always suffered a lot of pressure from both those above and the media whenever the big cases were on the go. Yet, despite that being so annoying at the time, it also provided the main drive and the much-needed adrenaline required to goad them on towards an eventual conclusion. Helen was starting to wonder about a possible promotion and how much longer she'd have to be stuck in the role of Inspector. She also had the likes of Cheryl Burgess chasing close on her heels, and that was starting to nag at her a little; not that she held any bad feelings towards the woman. She was a bright young thing who was certainly going places. The only trouble was it all took so bloody well long in this job, especially once you got caught up in the machine that drove the force forward on a budget that seemed to get tighter and tighter each year. That was the way it'd worked for many, many years. Everything had become so damned institutionalised, yet although that fact was known by all and sundry, it would still take a good long time for any changes to be made and for anyone to actually reap the benefits from any improvements they may make. As always, approvals for such things seemed to take forever and the good old red tape regime would eventually kick in once again. That was something the Brit's had been well renowned for down the centuries, and they still did it just as well even in today's so-called modern world.

*

'It had been one of those picturesque summer mornings in the Thames Ditton neighbourhood when the young mother, twenty-four-year-old Danielle Hinckley-Smith had cycled off to visit her mother who lived just ten minutes away in Longmead Road, having left her husband to look after the baby. She'd been dressed in a dark green T-shirt, a short black skirt and a pair of slip on beach shoes when she'd set off that Friday morning.

  It was about 9.45 and she'd cycled from their house in Embercourt Road to the direction of Western Green Road. The bike was a basic dark red Specialized brand with a shopping basket attached to the front which would have been holding her handbag, according to what her husband told us, having waved her off that morning. When she'd failed to return a few hours later, the husband had phoned his mother-in-law, only to be informed she'd never arrived. She'd just assumed something else had come up, as had happened on several occasions, so presumed her daughter would be along the next day instead. Therefore, she'd just sat and got engrossed in some soppy film on the TV.

  Naturally, Michael, Danielle's husband was immediately concerned and followed the route she would have taken, then drove all around the local area looking for her once he'd persuaded his next-door neighbour to babysit for him. Danielle's sister also happened to live fairly close by, so she also helped join the search. It was her who discovered the bike, but as there was no sign of Danielle, she became even more alarmed. That was when our local officers first received the call and began to get involved. A quick search of the area was carried out by ourselves, but at that point the whole thing was treated as more of a missing person's case.'

Liberty provided further details to the team whilst sat in her wheelchair, and they all listened knowing there was more to come.

'The turning point came when one of the officers found one of her shoes which the husband confirmed as being one his wife had been wearing when she'd left the house. As expected, a full search of the area then took place, although this failed to find anything further. The forensics team also visited the site along with Helen and Cheryl, whilst I was forced to stay back and watch from the main path, due to the limited accessibility of this wonderful contraption.' She stated, tapping its side, with most of the team not really sure how to react, but still managing to sense how frustrated she must have felt at the time.

'So right at this moment, as there's been no sign of a body or anything else to go on, we're treating this as a possible abduction and will be making further enquires in the area with door-to-door calls with an appeal for any witnesses in the local paper. There's also something planned to go out on the local news tonight, as we obviously need to move very quickly on this one, but I also need you to do what you usually do in such cases, and feedback any known perps in the area that you feel may have some bearing on this situation. Let's find

Danielle fast and get her back to her family as soon as possible. Are there any further questions from anyone?'

*

As instructed, and as part of the search and investigation into the suspected abduction of Danielle Hinckley-Smith, the twenty-four-year-old mother from Thames Ditton who'd gone missing, Cheryl and Helen worked one whole side of the street together during the door-to-door enquires. Knowing the importance of ensuring nothing was overlooked, they kept a close track on making sure none of the houses were missed and worked really well together. Cheryl did learn the valuable lesson that doorbells could be positioned in all sorts of crazy places. That made her recall a similar memory from the past regarding letterboxes when she'd been a youngster and had a job delivering morning newspapers before going to school in order to earn a bit of extra pocket money.

The response was much better than expected for that time of the week, especially with a whole batch of elderly people who'd all retired. They were all more than happy to chat, as they usually had very few visitors during the week. There were also quite a few mums and even a couple of stay-at-home dads with young kids who'd no doubt be at nursery or infant school at that time of the day. They'd obviously need dropping off and picking up of course, but with child care costs being so high these days, working wasn't even an option for some families any longer. Both women showed their ID's before asking the same set of questions with some taking a lot longer than others. The road they were in was quite a well sought-after, tree-lined avenue with a neighbourhood watch scheme in place that apparently ran much better than others in the area. That was down to whoever was coordinating it, according to the locals. It included the amount of time and dedication they could provide, and whether or not there were good turnouts at the meetings when held. Yet unfortunately, that only worked really well until they either lost interest or moved house.

It was always interesting from a trained policewoman's eye to see how bad the security was with some houses, plus you could always tell those who'd be gullible enough to fall for the numerous conmen who worked such areas. Some of the front gardens were highly impressive, although there were a couple that appeared rather unkempt in places and told you quite a bit about the occupants who lived there. A few others had building works going on and those required a bit of extra care when trying to negotiate crossing over to the front door. Those were the ones that could prove really deadly if you weren't paying proper attention.

Overall, the results were much the same and didn't turn up any new clues at first. In the meantime, Cheryl had another one of her hunches about something that'd been bouncing around in her head following one of the house calls. As a result, she was now extremely interested in pursuing the whole thing a little bit further.

*

Tom and Laken had happily agreed to babysit once more. His sister was more than happy to give them their own space, as she now had a relationship with a local man, even though it was in the early stages of development. He also had his own flat and was still working on the romantic charm offensive that would hopefully lead to him getting Ruth into bed.

With food consumed and the kids now hopefully sound asleep in their beds, Tom had already manoeuvred Laken so she now sat fully astride him on the sofa. He already had his hands up the inside of her new T-shirt while he worked hard and fast to drive her nipples to hardness between his thumbs and forefingers. Naturally, Laken was enjoying every moment and could already feel the hard-on beneath her as she closed her eyes and savoured the moment, thinking ahead to how he'd feel once he was deep inside her and banging away like a rampant rabbit on the home stretch.

Suddenly, without any warning, he caught a movement out of the corner of his eye, which instinctively informed Tom something wasn't quite right. He was certain they were no longer alone, but then, just to confirm his worst suspicion; Laken gave a short scream before collapsing forward onto him. Tom looked up then noticed Jenny standing over them with a composed smile on her face and a heavy looking paperweight held menacingly in her right hand.

'Looks like you really missed me lover boy. It's very possible your little plaything may be lucky enough to survive. It's just a real shame the same can't be said about you... you prize dickhead,' she cursed. Tom was desperately trying to roll Laken off him, but his girlfriend was a dead weight in her current state of unconsciousness. He was literally pinned down and totally unable to move in any direction. Under such circumstances, this made it ever so easy for Jenny to simply lean over and guide the needle deep into the side of his neck without so much as a struggle.

'Parting is such sweet sorrow.' Jenny quoted as she

waited a moment then repeatedly used the paperweight to smash in his skull. Blood splattered everywhere as the sickening sounds of flesh being destroyed along with bones being shattered, filled the room.

*

Cheryl had sat with Betty Tenant, a neighbour of the missing woman and consequently drunk more cups of tea than she remembered for a very long time. The old girl was clearly someone who craved company and probably had a good few visitors still. She'd talked about how her husband had died over twenty years ago and the fact that her only son had long since moved out to Australia, having met his future wife at university and followed her out when she'd grown homesick. Evidently, they'd married then had three children, and although she'd been invited to visit on a few occasions, Betty had never been brave enough to do so. It was sad to hear her story, but Cheryl was more than grateful she hadn't taken up the offer. Her hunch following the door-to-door calls had paid off from what she could tell so far.

Dear old Betty had just informed her about a young woman who'd mistakenly called at her house just over two-weeks ago and told her she'd been looking for Danielle. It sounded as if she'd known her quite well, but Cheryl knew this to be a typical trick used by criminals for years to gain knowledge about a neighbourhood before eventually committing a crime, which was usually a burglary or something of that nature.

Gaining a bit more data about how the woman had looked and sounded had been fairly hard work, as Betty had gone on to explain how her eyes and ears weren't quite as good as they used to be. That was before she added the rest of her entire medical history into the conversation. It sounded as if she'd suffered every possible ailment known to mankind and been to hell and back during that time. Of course, Cheryl had no choice but to act all sympathetic so as not to upset the poor woman, although there really were limits as to just how far you could go with some people.

After the umpteenth cup of tea and near to bursting, Cheryl had pretty much managed to gain everything she needed to know, when she stood up and made to leave. It was perfectly clear Betty didn't want her to go, but making up what she only deemed to be a small white lie, Cheryl convinced her it really was a matter of urgency, then finally managed to escape after having squeezed in a trip to the bathroom before doing so. What she hadn't expected however, was for Betty to hand her a small piece of note paper with a car number plate written down on it.

'That was the old car she'd driven off in? Betty informed her before shutting the door. Cheryl didn't even want to ask how someone who'd been complaining about having such bad eyesight a few minutes earlier had suddenly managed to deliver the goods. Right now, she just needed to catch up with Liberty and give her the latest news. No doubt that would provide her with a few more brownie points and make the team far happier than they had been.

Things really were going incredibly well at the moment, although the way her life tended to pan out, Cheryl was already wondering when the cracks would start to appear and send her career spiralling off in a downward direction.

*

Awake in both mind and body, Helen had been feeling incredibly peckish from the moment she'd opened her eyes to greet another day. Now she stood in the kitchen with two deliciously looking thick slices of toast, both fully laden with poached eggs and a whole cluster of mushrooms she'd had left over from the day before, but couldn't possibly dream of wasting.

Sitting at the small dining room table, which more than ably served its purpose, Helen sat watching the breakfast news on the TV. This was fixed to a swivel wall bracket that allowed her to view the screen from wherever she sat, and was one of the better ideas she'd had about the place. The bonus of having it that way was she was also able to twist it around to see it from the open plan kitchen if need be.

She fed her face and knew the likelihood of eating again at lunchtime wasn't always what'd be classed as a clear-cut event in her profession. Every day was different and in her type of job you seriously never knew what was likely to be hiding just around the corner or getting ready to pounce at any time. Grabbing up the remote to change channels, as the male anchor-man in the newsroom was the one that really annoyed her at the best of times; Helen was much more satisfied with the BBC coverage. She always felt their programmes presented themselves with a much more proficient and professional slant, as well as avoiding ten ton of crappy commercials.

Dan Walker was the man. He was certainly much more pleasing on the eye than the pasty looking joker on the other side who thought his own wise cracks were amusing. Evidently Dan was really tall in real life, which made quite a bit of sense when she considered it further. She recalled him interviewing a few footballers pitch-side on the TV. They'd come across as being quite small; either that or they must have been standing in a hole. Helen had just literally swallowed the last mouthful of food from her plate when her mobile went off. She immediately answered to the sound of Liberty asking her to make her way into work sooner rather than later.

'I was just about to leave as soon as I'd brushed my teeth boss. Is everything alright or has some sort of breakthrough happened?' She listened to the reply and after hanging up and switching off the television; she shot up the stairs, sorted out her teeth and was out of the house within the space of six minutes. The fact that Liberty had told her she'd fill her in once she arrived, already told her she had some important news.

Naturally, her enquiring mind was already racing away and imagining all kinds of different scenarios as she drove along, although that did mean she wasn't taking in much of what was going on around her. Already in automaton mode and having done the same journey so many times before, it only took her fifteen minutes to get there, even though the traffic was relatively busy. Once parked and bounding up the back stairs two at a time, Helen entered through the door leading directly into her department and rushed straight to where Liberty sat dead still in her wheelchair, busily staring at the screen on her computer.

'Based on what Cheryl discovered from her follow-up with that old lady on the door-to-door calls you'd done together out on the knock, and added to the fact we've only just been informed that Jenny Manson managed to escape prison a few weeks ago, my gut feeling was something really bad was about to happen. So true to what I was thinking, we now have this,' Liberty affirmed, as they both peered at the image on the screen.

'That means Jenny's out for revenge and really means business again.' The monitor displayed a call that had come in, and requested a visit to a house near Chessington.

Apparently, the blood splattered body of a victim by the name of Tom Jones had been discovered by his girlfriend who'd been incredibly lucky to have survived the entire onslaught.

'Oh, for goodness sake! That's Jenny's ex... We need to get over there fast,' Helen exclaimed with her fingernails making a series of indentations in the top of the wheelchair she'd been holding onto rather too tightly during the viewing.

'I'm so pleased you waited for me Lib's, but this whole thing's absolutely crazy. What the hell are we up against for fuck sake? Forget ISO Killer, I'm honestly starting to believe Jenny Manson's the devil in disguise.'

Minutes later, with Liberty's wheelchair loaded within record time, the DCI was already putting her foot down on the accelerator with the blue lights flashing as she pulled out of the car park. She negotiated several of the roads she needed to tackle, then flew down the A3 before taking the next junction off, much to the annoyance of the drivers she'd managed to cut up.

CHAPTER 19

Fear took hold of Danielle once again, as she heard the woman return and gave up struggling just before she entered the room. She looked to be on some sort of high as she was moving around and talking much faster than previously. Jenny removed the tape from Danielle's mouth to feed her and give her water to drink, which meant she wanted to keep her alive for now. Once finished, Danielle pleaded with her to keep the tape from her mouth. This seemed to be something the woman considered, but then just stood staring at her. That was when Danielle spotted what looked like large amounts of blood all over her skin and clothing, and that freaked her out even more.

Jenny was still buzzing from murdering Tom. She needed some sort of release and gazed down at her captive knowing she was able to do whatever she wanted. The woman was at her mercy and the whole reason for her capture, had been to get back at her for acting so snobbish in the court room. She was probably around about the same age, she guessed. She looked much prettier now, and had a nice face with generous lips with blue eyes that appeared quite sparkly, even in that darkened room.

Jenny walked over and adjusted one of the worn-out curtains to allow extra light in, to gain a better look. Danielle's hair was a blondish colour which rather surprisingly, had a slightly red tint to it. This made Jenny wonder if she'd possibly judged the woman all wrong, before her eyes edged down to her long sun-tanned legs and noticed her short skirt had ridden up to reveal the edge of a pair of black lacy knickers. An image of her and Lana lying naked together entered her mind and an urge for release suddenly kicked in.

Danielle was completely helpless to do anything about what was happening, as her abductor set about freeing her legs first and then removing the tape that had bound them to each of the chair legs. At first, she assumed she was being released, but then the woman started to reach up and remove her underwear, before eventually taping her legs back up again.

Danielle had had no idea what was going on, at least not until Jenny stepped back and then started to strip off all her own clothes, whilst studying her face for any sign of reaction. Standing stark naked before her just moments later, the woman suddenly started to tease her own nipples until they'd fully hardened. Then she reached down and worked her fingers around her vaginal area, before inserting her finger and starting to moan with pleasure.

Danielle simply stared and watched with fascination. She'd never had any lesbian tendencies or even given it a thought when going through school, despite the fact she'd known such things had gone on amongst some of the girls. Now however, for reasons totally alien to her, she felt herself getting all wet down below as she continued to watch the figure's fingers moving in and out, with her own wetness running down her legs. The woman had completely lost all sense of her inhibitions and was moaning so loudly. Jenny continued rubbing and was trying to climax with traces of sticky liquid in her hand, which she'd collected on purpose to use on Danielle.

*

Rowena had started becoming aware of the strange brown patch in the ceiling tiles just above her desk a few weeks back, and it definitely appeared to be getting worse with each passing day. With this day being a particularly hot one with the windows opened due to the air conditioning being so crap, quite a few flies had gathered and seemed to be especially interested in that same spot all of a sudden. As she sat and studied them closer, Rowena realised the faint smell that had been bothering her, had become a whole lot stronger and was almost certainly coming from the same place.

She'd already spoken to the office manager, who'd reported it to the facilities management team that worked for the landlord. Yet despite chasing it up a few times, nothing had been forthcoming. Whatever prompted her to do what she'd decided to go and do that day, would always remain a mystery to everyone who'd been working in that office. With Rowena being Rowena, and in conjunction with her intolerance regarding things not getting done on time, she'd promptly disappeared into the cleaner's cupboard, grabbed the nearest broom, and then set about poking the area around the damp patch with it.

What happened next, stayed etched in the minds of those who witnessed the ceiling collapse. It revealed the rotting body of what was clearly a female, and it landed across two of the desks below, whilst causing an unbelievable mess that came with a stench that made it so much worse.

Rowena had worked as a volunteer in the local police station for many years and recalled one of the detectives explaining how a body instantly starts turning cold once the hearts finally stopped. The first period was something she'd never forget. That was more commonly known as the death chill; or at least it was until the body heat finally dropped to room temperature. As there was no longer any movement or circulation to keep the blood moving through the body, that would start to pool together and settle for up to two to six hours, depending on certain conditions. From that point on, the body would start to grow all stiff with rigor mortis setting in. Although the body was dead, there were still all manner of organisms living in the intestines with other things like skin cells within the body that were still alive. These could still be harvested then fed on by the likes of flesh flies before leading to the eventual putrefaction, or decomposition of the body.

Despite the fact his trusting colleague, Sue truly believed the sun shone out of Peter's backside, there was now no doubting Peter Satterthwaite has buried his wife under the floorboards in the office above his work and known he'd be caught in due course.

When the case eventually reached court, it turned out the man was incredibly vindictive and felt that would be a great way to get back at the work colleagues who constantly pissed him off.

A call was made, but with her and Helen already on their way to the scene of Tom's death, Liberty decided to pass it to her team to deal with, and insisted that they included Cheryl on that one. The experience would do them good, plus it would allow her to find out how they managed to handle it on their own for a change.

*

By the time they reached Tom's sisters house, the local police; a male and two females who'd arrived there first, having responded as soon as the call came in, had already determined there was no need for medical assistance as Tom was well and truly dead. They'd been very careful not to disturb anything and confirmed the murderer who'd fled the scene as the deceased's ex.

The woman who survived was apparently his latest girlfriend. She'd witnessed her leaving, but despite being in a certain state of shock, had still recognised her from something Tom had once shown her.

'Her?' queried Liberty, staring straight at Helen with her senses screaming ten to the gallon inside her head.

'Yes,' confirmed Helen, looking straight back. Chris Bradley, the male officer, informed them the girlfriend's name was Laken and was currently sitting in the room next door with his partner Kelly. He also explained that Tina, a second female officer also on the scene, was busy upstairs with two young kids by the names of Matthew and Katie. They were aged seven and five respectively and their mother, Ruth, had already been contacted and was on her way back home, although she hadn't been told the whole story about her brother having been killed just yet.

As instructed, Chris took all the required steps to protect the house and ensure it was secure by isolating the crime scene with tape stored in the boot of his patrol car. He then stood guard to ensure he stopped any unauthorised personnel from entering the house until it had been properly investigated, or until Liberty as the lead investigator told him what he needed to do next. Chris knew from police training that physical evidence could easily be rendered useless by anyone wandering through the area. Anyone, including him and his two colleagues, were more than capable of destroying valuable evidence without even realising.

Donald Raggett arrived with the forensics team and set about doing what they needed to do for the collection of evidence. Liberty had already conducted an initial walk-through of the scene and worked out what had happened, including how she saw it from the killer's point of view.

Now she accompanied Don for a second look, although this time the aim was to maintain the integrity of any evidence they needed to collect, while his team took photographs of the entire scene and surrounding areas, which included the blood splattered walls as well as points of entry and exit. They also collected minute traces of blood and dust, with fibres for later examination in their laboratory, whilst following the strict packaging guidelines in order to prevent any contamination of the evidence. This was very much needed, especially as blood was prone to growing mould if packaged when wet, so therefore it always required to be air dried first.

As always, Don promised to provide Liberty and her team with the full report once the autopsy was completed, although they'd both concluded the deceased had initially been injected in the neck with a paralysing drug before having his head smashed to a pulp with the paperweight.

It was a shame the girlfriend hadn't witnessed the

actual attack. She'd been out cold, having been struck in the first instance by the exact same murder weapon. Thankfully, Laken had confirmed Jenny Manson as the killer when shown a more recent photo by Helen, and although it hadn't been necessary, Jenny obviously wanted to leave her trade mark by using the syringe to ensure they knew it was her.

So, how the hell had she managed to escape prison and what was she up to now?

*

Just as expected, the naked woman immediately moved in front of her and forced her skirt up as far as she could. At first, she'd just crouched there on her knees, playing with her own nipples and watching intently with a smile on her face until she confirmed Danielle was wet. She then inserted her finger and worked on her, while her mouth hung open with her tongue out, as if trying to tease her. Danielle's body just reacted as expected. Within a matter of minutes, Jenny had lowered her face into her captive's pubic bush and worked her tongue around with great expertise, knowing exactly which points to hit. Despite Danielle trying her best to fight it, love juice came pouring out and Jenny just allowed it to run over her face, her hair and then work its way down her chest between her bare breasts. Danielle moaned and orgasmed like she never had before, then felt guilty she'd actually enjoyed the whole experience. She watched as the woman stood up and then mouthed a *thank you* before walking from the room with an insane grin on her face. That was the moment recognition finally dawned on her with Danielle suddenly recognising Jenny Manson as the woman she'd helped send down in court. Now she sat in absolute turmoil having completely forgotten what had just occurred.

She was in the hands of a ruthless killer who'd been described as completely cold-hearted, insensitive to anyone's feelings, and someone with a mind full of nothing but cruelness and pure evil. Maybe what had just taken place was all part of a plan, and her way of degrading her just before going in for the kill.

*

Laken was a very attractive Maltese woman with long blond hair and Helen couldn't help thinking she resembled Jenny Manson in some strange way. Tom must have felt his luck was on a roll when first encountering her at his sister's house, although that certainly wasn't the case right now. It was obvious Laken had truly fancied Tom and felt quite serious about him, and she'd also been very honest and open about them using the babysitting to have sex. That made Helen think about Mark for a fleeting moment, and then realised how much she missed him, even if it was just for a nice cuddle and the feeling of being wanted by someone who loved you.

They were soon back at the station with Laken now making a formal statement. Everything was being taped with notes written down and both women drinking much needed coffees. They felt quite at ease in each other's presence and Laken had already had her head wound treated, along with a promise to speak up and say something if she felt faint or had any sign of a headache emerging. She still needed to be careful for a while, but at least Helen was aware and keeping a good eye on her.

The paramedic who'd treated her from the back of an ambulance outside Ruth's house, the same one that had arrived as part of the call-out to collect Tom's body, had told her she was incredibly lucky as it could have been a different story if the paperweight had caught her in the temple. It had only needed to be another half-inch away from where it had struck. He'd also informed her there'd be no long-term markings once her wound had a decent chance to heal, although she'd have to be patient in letting it do so. All in all, Laken was the sort of witness the police service preferred, and she was extremely helpful in confirming Jenny's identity. It transpired that Tom had carried a picture of his ex in his wallet and shown it to Laken just before he'd destroyed it and then replaced it with the photograph that she'd given him of herself.

Ruth had arrived just before they'd left the house. Naturally, she'd taken her brother's death extremely badly, but they had managed to calm her down in the end, before packing her and the two kids off to a close friend, who just happened to live a few doors away, and was more than happy to help out.

As protocol dictated, the house needed to be closed off as a crime scene for a while. That also gave them a chance to say farewell to Chris, Kelly and Tina, whose shifts were about to finish once their replacements turned up to take over. Fortunately, that was happening just before she, Liberty and Laken headed off back to the station.

*

Not long after they'd returned, a call to Liberty from Don Raggett confirmed exactly what they'd been expecting to hear. Succinylcholine chloride was corroborated as having been the drug injected into Tom's neck as per Jenny Manson's so-called trademark. Her identity had been backed up even further by the fingerprints taken from the paperweight and a few other places on the way both in and out of the house. A lack of gloves didn't mean she'd been careless, it just meant the woman was past caring any longer. That now changed things a bit, and made her incredibly dangerous. It also meant she was probably very unstable in the head and therefore unpredictable in whatever she was up too right now. They'd have to be extra vigilant from now on, so Liberty made a mental note to ensure she notified every member of her team.

Don had gone over the remaining findings just to make sure she'd been given the full details, but there were no great surprises to be conveyed. Liberty thanked him for the update, and he promised the relevant paperwork would be with her as soon as possible, before the call finally ended.

Liberty sat and thought carefully about the whole case from the very beginning to the point they were at right now. Her shining star, Cheryl had come up trumps yet again, by detecting the missing woman, Danielle Hinckley-Smith had been part of the jury at the Jenny Manson case eight months ago. She was now busy trying to track down the whereabouts of a car she felt Jenny may have been using, yet the real question was whether or not Danielle was still alive. If that was so, where was she being held and what sort of state would the poor woman be in? Jenny certainly didn't have a great track record for showing any signs of tolerance or respect for human life from what they'd seen so far. So, where the hell was she likely to be hiding out right now?

The DCI reached over for her cup and hoped a swig of strong coffee might set the old brain cells working in the right direction. Times like this were among the most frustrating parts of the job, and there was nothing much you could do apart from hope and pray that something would turn up sooner rather than later. Every second really did count, and time certainly wasn't on Danielle Hinckley-Smith's side right now.

CHAPTER 20

Cheryl Burgess was having another one of her *good days*, or at least that was how it appeared for now. Liberty had asked her to chase up on the car number plate to see what else she could come up with, and was now convinced Jenny Manson was the woman who'd called in on Betty as part of a ploy to get to Danielle Hinckley-Smith. Working from the description Betty had provided her with, this also meant she'd changed her hair by cutting it a lot shorter, thus making her appear a lot more boyish, or so she assumed.

Showing up on the screen before her, was a record of a ticket dished out by a traffic cop for a car with the same registration just a few days ago for having a broken rear light on the left-hand side. Hitting the keypad enthusiastically, Cheryl felt the adrenaline start to kick in as she was sure she was on the right track, while jotting down the necessary details that included the officers contact details. She rung straight away and was evidently very lucky to find him in, as he'd just arrived back at the station. Sure enough, she realised she'd hit the jackpot when she came off the phone all excited just ten minutes later and felt things were definitely going her way.

The officer in question had confirmed the driver as having been female and matching Jenny's description almost perfectly. Apparently, she'd been driving under a completely different name, plus he'd confirmed there were only a handful of houses out in the direction she'd been heading for. He'd never seen her around the area before, or at least he certainly didn't recall having done so, but according to local town gossip, the old house out towards the old ruined windmill where Mable Finch had died from old age had been rented out to a young woman by the rental company a few years back. She was said to be a real recluse, and if it was the same woman, that would explain why he hadn't seen her before.

Having provided her with the remaining details she'd requested and wishing her the best of luck with whatever it was she was looking into, Cheryl immediately followed up the call with another one to the managing agents and asked to be put through to the branch manager.

Everything was finally slotting into place at long last, and it wasn't long after, before she was straight back on the phone giving Liberty a complete rundown of her latest findings.

*

Mentally, Danielle wasn't even sure where she stood any longer. Jenny had abused her twice more, and although she'd known it was totally wrong, she'd still been sexually excited and actually enjoyed the experience. What also went through her head was the fact she was still living and breathing, whereas she'd fully expected to be dead by now. Although, that was solely based on her abductors track record and what she'd evidenced during the court case against her. Danielle felt Jenny had been fantasising and had a bit of a girl crush on her, especially as she'd heard her use the name Lana at one time; not that she spoke very often. She was being fed and watered quite regularly, which she also saw as a good sign, but she did feel rather dirty. Danielle had always prided herself on cleanliness, but the water being used to clean her up after each session was always horribly cold. This logically made her think there was no hot water to be had, and what with the place being so old, dark and dingy, Danielle figured out they were probably in the middle of nowhere, which made the odds of her chances of being found much worse than she'd hoped. She just prayed the police were on the ball and got to her on time. Hopefully it would be the same woman she'd seen in court with the name that sounded really cool for a detective, although she really couldn't recall what it had been. Danielle knew she'd have to try her best to keep Jenny happy for the time being. Pissing her off really wasn't an option, although being tied to the chair had become increasingly painful with the binds on her wrists and ankles having grown quite sore where they'd been rubbing against her bare skin. She'd have to say something soon, but maybe she just needed to work out the best way to phrase it and ask at the right time.

The whole thing was an absolute nightmare. The poor woman was really missing her family and *so* wanted to see them again. Tears started to run down Danielle's cheeks as she pictured them all, and swore if she managed to survive, she'd ensure she always appreciated what she had in life and make the most of every single day.

*

Back at the station, every member of the team gathered for the emergency meeting that Liberty had called. They were all aware there'd been a breakthrough, but now they were about to hear the details first-hand, and then be told what the next plan of action would be. There was a great buzz of excitement amongst them and the whole atmosphere was completely changed from that of the last gathering, where everyone had seemed so down in the dumps.

Once she'd managed to gain everyone's attention and the room had quietened down, Liberty spoke out loud and provided them the guidance of a true leader. She was assured they'd bring Jenny Manson to justice and make sure she was banged up for evermore this time around.

Liberty not only exuded confidence, but worked to install it in every member of her team as well. All the latest updates were fully relayed as expected, with the necessary alterations made to the picture board with photographs and any associated records passed around to ensure everyone was singing off the same hymn sheet. An overall action plan was provided with names given to specific tasks that nobody had any issues with. Every person in that room realised how important each assigned role would be in gaining the end result. The fact that Detective Superintendent Heather Palmer also entered the room five minutes into the meeting, also added to the importance of the whole thing.

'Let me just remind you that you're the best Major Investigation Team out of the four that currently exist within the Specialist Crime and Operation Directorate right now. I'm incredibly proud of each and every one of you and I'm well aware not everything's been plain sailing. I'll leave you in the more than capable hands of Liberty and Helen, as I should have been in another meeting a few minutes ago. Good luck on this one, and let's get the result we're looking for.'

Heather turned and left the room to a couple of cheers before Helen took the floor and went on to provide a few additional facts, before answering a couple of burning questions that needed to be sorted once the meeting had officially ended.

*

Liberty and Helen left the car and edged towards the house with extreme caution. They were looking for an old detached house according to the letting agency and this certainly didn't disappoint. It was more than run down with large patches of green moss and black mould covering the outside walls that gave it a much more sinister look than it deserved. The door and window frames looked more than desperate for a lick of paint and Helen couldn't help thinking what the place may have looked like with some proper TLC.

It was pretty awkward for Liberty's wheelchair to negotiate the garden as the weeds were so overgrown in places. The long, thorny, arching shoots of brambles sprung out from everywhere and were doing their best to snag at her. But Helen came to the rescue and managed to push her boss over and onto the main decking, although that also looked like a right death-trap, especially as it was so obviously in need of repair

225

in places. They gradually moved around to the rear end of the building and tried to be as quiet as possible; despite that not being something they'd managed too well so far. Both women stopped and paused for breath then listened carefully before Helen tried out the back door to see if it would open. Fortunately, it gave, as luck appeared to be on their side for a change. It may have been unlocked due to the place being so remote, but the two detectives were well aware it could also be a trap.

Liberty had already gained the okay for the two of them to go it alone with Heather's full backing. She felt a full hit squad descending on the house would have placed Danielle's life in greater jeopardy by going in too heavy handed. At least this way there may be room for negotiation if Jenny happened to be in a listening mood.

Once her wheelchair had negotiated the steps at the back door and enabled her to follow Helen inside, Liberty found the interior to be incredibly dark due to the curtains all being drawn. It was also very damp and musty smelling, although this was no surprise as not a single window had been open, according to what they'd seen outside.

'I'll search the upstairs if you look around down here boss. Just be careful. Jenny's a ruthless killer and it doesn't help to know we're probably at the top of her hit-list.' Liberty returned the remark about being careful as she watched her partner ascend the stairs and felt helpless that she couldn't do more.

*

There was a great feeling of relief once her eyes settled on Danielle Hinckley-Smith tied to a high-backed

226

wooden chair. She was sitting with a gag around her mouth as Helen entered what she'd assumed was the main bedroom, despite there being very little furniture around. The woman was alive and appeared to look quite well. She didn't seem to be drugged either, but suddenly Helen noticed her eyes go wide as if she were trying to tell her something.

Seconds later, Helen lay on her back and winced with pain as she tried to open her eyes and take in her surroundings. What she hadn't allowed for was the glare of the bare lightbulb shining overhead with a brightness that was so intense, it messed with her efforts to regain some form of normality. Yet that discomfort almost paled into significance in comparison to the searing pain she felt coming from the back of her head. It felt as if it were penetrating her very soul.

Once her vision gradually cleared and allowed her to take in the full picture, Helen felt very self-conscious that she'd allowed herself to end up as she had, and then managed to get into the whole situation in the first place. Gently raising herself up on her elbows and overcoming the wave of nausea trying to overwhelm her, she eventually managed to sit up but was more than surprised to find Danielle still sitting tied up, fully alive and gazing down at her.

Reaching down and removing a tissue from her jacket pocket, Helen did her best to clean herself up and take time to recover a bit more. Despite finding traces of blood on the tissue having applied it to the back of her head then checking it out, Helen knew it wasn't as bad as it could have been. She sat back to allow her body to recuperate further rather than rushing off and making things ten times worse, but as her thoughts settled back down and allowed her some form of normality, Helen cast her mind back to what had happened to leave her in such a state in the first place. She vaguely recalled looking back following Danielle's warning with a shadowy figure suddenly appearing behind her, then striking her with something hard before everything went all blurry, and she'd lost consciousness.

Liberty...Oh Bloody Hell! In a moment of panic, Inspector Helen Morgan threw any thoughts of caution to the wind and got straight to her feet. She was well aware her balance wouldn't be brilliant just yet, but moving to the doorway at the far end of the room, she called out for Liberty as loudly as she could. She'd given Danielle an apologetic look that said she didn't have time to untie her right now as something more urgent came first.

Just as she was about to look in the second of the downstairs rooms, a muffled sound came from one of the cupboards just over to her right. Reaching over and yanking it open with one quick jerk, Helen wasn't quite sure whether to laugh or cry at the image of her boss totally jammed inside the tiny cupboard whilst seated in her wheelchair. The woman cursed for England as the light from the torch suddenly flooded in and she realised how ridiculous she must have looked.

'Get me out of this stupid box so we can get after that bloody nutcase.' She cursed. But setting Liberty free wasn't as easy as expected. The wheelchair had been jammed in very tightly with hardly any give on either side. Fortunately, only one of the walls was made of brick with the other being mostly plasterboard. With a bit of manipulation and sheer brute force, the weaker side suddenly gave way, shooting them both out of the cupboard and back into the hallway. At that point they both started to laugh. It was more out of relief but only lasted for a brief moment as the seriousness of the situation kicked back in. Helen then shot upstairs to free Danielle before they were able to continue their search for Jenny.

*

Helen was completely shocked to find the chair empty when she got there. The ties had been discarded on the floor and that could only mean Jenny must have returned and taken Danielle with her. Why on earth would she have done that? Maybe Jenny felt something for her. In that instance, Helen realised that made sense and possibly explained why she and Liberty were still alive. Jenny had obviously been caught unprepared. Now her plan, assuming she had one, would be right up in the air. Just as Helen arrived back downstairs, the sound of a car engine trying to start up echoed outside.

Moving across to the car, Jenny spotted them both come out then slammed her hand hard on the steering wheel as she realised they'd disabled it before entering the house. Knowing she'd be unable to escape with Danielle alongside; Jenny left the woman stuffed inside the boot and tried to block out her screams before rushing away.

'You get after her, and I'll check to see if Danielle's alright.' Liberty ordered, just as Helen set off after the fleeing figure.

Helen was moving faster than Jenny and quickly made up ground as she cut across the drive and launched herself at the woman desperately trying to make a quick getaway. Attacking her had been a real gamble. She never knew if she'd be armed with a knife or anything. Helen knew it was all about getting the timing perfectly right and luck appeared to be on her side as her shoulder crashed into Jenny's back and sent her sprawling across the yard before landing face down on the concrete path. Luckily, Helen managed to maintain her balance so she moved across to keep a close eye on the killer, who appeared to be knocked unconscious.

Unfortunately for her, Jenny was obviously much tougher than expected. As soon as she looked back towards the car to check out how Liberty was faring, Jenny suddenly sprung to life, shot back up into a standing position and then charged straight at her. Helen had no choice but to try and protect herself from the attack by hitting out with an instinctive hard right as soon as Jenny drew close enough. Her luck didn't hold up however, as Jenny simply blocked the punch and immediately hit back by landing a blow that knocked Helen sideways before leaning over and picking up a hefty lump of broken branch from the ground. She swung it hard with all her weight behind it and caught Helen in her ribcage with a force that completely knocked the wind from the policewoman's lungs. Trying her best to draw breath and knowing she didn't have much time to recover, Helen suddenly slipped on something underfoot as Jenny swung the branch at her again. She gave out a look of anguish as she automatically stuck her right arm up to protect herself, then screamed as it made full contact with the lump of wood. There was a distinct sound of breaking bone that echoed in the air and sounded quite ugly. Jenny knew she had the upper hand as she followed this up by whacking Helen in the back of the legs, spun around, dropped the branch then rushed back towards the house and disappeared inside.

*

It wasn't an easy task, but Liberty had done her bit to help Danielle from the back of the car and was checking she was unharmed when they heard a loud crack. It was the pretty distinctive sound of a limb being broken, and they both winced at the pain involved as they stared over and saw Helen go down.

Liberty had never moved so fast. Having caught sight of the figure fleeing in the distance, she'd instructed Danielle to check out Helen for her, then set off in her wheelchair towards the house whilst fully determined to catch the killer. As she travelled across the bumpy ground, her handbag slipped from the wheelchair, but she just carried on, as every second counted.

Entering the house, Liberty shouted for Jenny to come to her senses.

'Back-up's on its way. Danielle's safe and there's nowhere for you to run too.' She emphasised. There were countless noises inside the creaky old house, any of which could have been Jenny moving around. Liberty's senses may have been heightened, but she was still feeling far too exposed and a little scared. If she'd been fully mobile it would have been a different story altogether, but she was damned if she'd back down because of her disability. She was either a very brave cop or a completely stupid one.

Then, just as she was electing what the best approach would be, she became aware of another presence in the room and realised Jenny had managed to creep up behind her. Expecting to be struck at any moment, Liberty was quite surprised the woman gave her time to turn and face her.

'My life was messed up at a very early age, but you fucked it up even further when you decided to stick your nose into my business.' Jenny told her.

'Well you can't just go around killing people wherever and whenever you wish. There are consequences in this world and you're no different from anyone else out there,' she responded.

What happened next was all a bit of a blur, yet it all seemed to be over in a flash.

Jenny was just about to inject Liberty in the neck with the syringe when she suddenly stiffened and her eyes went wide with shock. At first it looked as if she was having a fit of some kind as her body began to tremble in a rather bizarre way, but then blood suddenly started dribbling from the corners of her mouth before she fell forward and crashed to the floor. She'd caught the top of the wheelchair on the way down and spun it around leaving Liberty to try and sum up what the hell had just happened.

She hadn't realised what had been happening at first. She'd felt a sharp prick to the left side of her neck when Jenny had been holding her in a vice-like grip, but that had been just before everything had gone totally crazy. Gazing down again, she knew Jenny Manson was dead before staring back up and noticing Danielle standing beside her in a state of shock. Liberty noticed she held what she could only assume was one of her knitting needles clutched tightly in her hand, and the whole thing was dripping with blood. The poor woman must have taken it from the handbag she'd dropped outside. Liberty had kept meaning to remove them because they were the new size 3's she'd recently purchased for the double-knit jumper she was planning to make for

Helen's birthday in two-months' time. The DCI knew it was wrong, yet she was laughing deep inside as she sensed the old saying *'He who lives by the sword shall die by the sword,'* madly shooting around inside her head. Although this time it happened to be a needle rather than a sword.

EPILOGUE

As expected, Danielle Hinckley-Smith suffered quite badly from the entire experience. It took her a good long while to get back to what most people would have classed as some form of reasonable normality. She'd undergone numerous sessions of counselling and been so happy to be back with her husband and the baby, who seemed to have grown quite a bit since she'd last seen her.

Danielle's mother had also taken her abduction very badly and even blamed herself for a while, seeing as her daughter had been cycling over to see her when she'd gone missing. She hadn't been in the best of health to start with, which resulted in her having to be admitted to hospital while the whole saga continued. Happily, she was now back at home and they'd set up carers to visit her twice a day because her daughter wasn't quite up to taking on such a responsibility in her current state of mind.

Danielle still felt deeply humiliated from what happened in the house and was quite ashamed at how her own feelings had come about during the whole encounter. She'd not allowed her husband to have sex with her since she'd returned home, so that was causing quite a strain along with the never-ending stream of press coverage and TV interviews that proved to be part and package of the complete media circus that revolved around the case.

At twenty-four years old, Danielle still had her whole life ahead of her, but it was definitely proving to be quite an uphill battle for now.

*

Had she still been alive, Serena Mack, her two boys and her gorgeous girl, who she'd always called her Little Princess, would have moved to Woodbridge in East Anglia in order to start a new life and escape the fact that her ex-husband, Peter Satterthwaite could be such a Jekyll and Hyde character. She'd already started planning this, but sadly she'd never had a chance to fully see it through.

Peter had eventually been tried for the murder of his wife, and the kids had ended up going to live with Serena's parents, who'd always adored them but constantly nagged at her to leave her husband, as they'd never really liked him from the very first instant, they'd met him.

'His eyes are far too close together for my liking,' her dad had always told her, yet she'd just laughed it off and put it down to one of those silly superstitious things people of their age seemed to believe in.

Peter Satterthwaite was sentenced to life imprisonment for Serena's murder and his work colleague, Rowena proved to be as tough as old boots. She was never really all that phased about the fact his wife's rotting body had decorated her work desk for a while, in fact she seemed to gain great delight in telling the story and even appeared to have turned the whole thing into some sort of joke.

His other colleague, Sue Johnson who'd always had a crush on him and seriously believed the man could do no wrong in her eyes, finally realised she probably wasn't really the greatest judge of character when it came to men. Her private life sort of confirmed that to be the case, but Peter's replacement wasn't too bad looking, and she would have sworn he'd made eyes at her last Tuesday afternoon in the staff kitchen.

*

Helen was finally patched up, although it took much longer than expected for her broken arm to recover, due to the fact that she was constantly moving around. She wouldn't rest as ordered and generally proved to be a pain in the backside until she was able to get herself back to normal at work.

Heather had called both her and Cheryl into the office one morning with Liberty sitting in attendance, and although they both wondered what they'd done wrong by being summoned as they had, both women were congratulated for doing such a good job during their part in the 'ISO Killer' murders, as per the name that'd been adopted by everyone. Off the record, Jenny Manson had suffered nothing more than she'd deserved, although she had managed to screw plenty of people's lives up along the way. There'd always be members of the public who'd be adamant she never had a good start in life. But their job was to uphold the law and not allow the Jenny's of this world to walk around believing they were above the law and allowed to do whatever they pleased.

Therefore, as a result of their dedication, and having

both proved their worth during that and a good few other cases, Heather had decided to promote the two of them forthwith.

*

Liberty was not so lucky at first. That was because Heather had given her a bit of a dressing down for placing herself in such danger and acting so gung-ho.

'This case has made me realise I can't afford to lose my best DCI. I personally took an exceptionally huge gamble, despite there being a good deal of pressure coming down from above.

The whole idea of you being out there in that wheelchair was a bit of an unknown to all of us, and to be honest with you Lib's, I'm really not prepared to let that happen again. I know you'll be disappointed and extremely frustrated, but at the same time, I can assure you that I had to go through the exact same thing when my days on the outside came to a halt and left me pen-pushing behind this desk. I guess what I'm telling you is... lead the team from in here, and then let the younger one's do the rest.'

Liberty just sat trying to take it all in at first. She knew Heather was right in what she was saying, but actually hearing it being said was surprisingly scary. It wasn't all bad news however, as a few days later, Liberty was presented with the powered wheelchair she'd been promised and fitted up for a while ago. The Ocean Blue F3 Corpus front wheel drive wheelchair had four wheels that touched the ground in a dreamlike fashion. It ran off a Group 34 Gel battery with various charging options that would easily suit her life both at work and at home.

Best of all was the joystick control that provided a fully

powered, movable leg rest with tilt repositioning and a seat elevation to allow her to move up and down. That meant she could finally reach her damned fridge and all those items that eluded her in shops with their high up shelves.

Watch out world, Liberty Rock will be back with a vengeance, she thought.

*

Going against all the principles she'd managed to sustain for such a long time, Lana had been as good as glued to the regular news broadcasts and even found herself flicking between channels, ever since the day Jenny Manson had gone off and left her. Now her lovely face was showing up all over the place as newsreaders and reporters ranted on about: all the killings she'd committed, how she'd been dubbed 'The ISO Killer', the sentence she'd received, her escape, how she'd tracked down and murdered her ex-boyfriend, plus Danielle Hinckley-Smith's abduction along with the attempted murder of a police women.

The latest images showed graphic close-ups of her dead body as they continued to talk about her death with such jubilation. It all sounded so damned sick and final that Lana couldn't help but weep. She felt incredibly low as reports continued to pour in one after another. They'd never really understood the true woman inside Jenny. They'd never even bothered to try for that matter. To them, she was just another one of life's miserable failures who was better off dead with the streets allegedly being much safer without the likes of people like her wandering around.

At one point, when the news had first broken, Lana

had dug out an old pistol her father had once used during his army days so long ago. She'd kept it carefully hidden away in the loft all wrapped up in newspaper and stored inside an old cardboard box. So, having finally decided to end it once and for all, once she'd realised how deep her love for Jenny had been, Lana had literally put the gun to her head and decided to pull the trigger.

Yet, something nagging inside the woman had stopped her dead in her tracks as she visualised the whole scene with her body lying sprawled across the floor and a river of blood gushing from a deep hole in the side of her head with traces of brain dotted everywhere. Deciding that was nothing short of a coward's way out, and not the prettiest of sights for whoever would have to finally clean it all up, Lana had a much better idea instead.

During the short space of time they'd been together, she and Jenny had managed to discuss a great many things. In some ways they'd appeared very similar, especially regarding the crappy lives they'd both led from a very early age. She realised Jenny wouldn't have wanted her to waste her life by committing suicide, but she'd certainly loved to have watched her go out and gain revenge.

Grabbing a nice cool bottle of cider from the fridge, along with the pen and paper she picked up from the sideboard, Lana sat back down in front of the screen and waited for the name of the DCI to be mentioned once again.

'I'll see you again soon Jenny my love. I've just got a few things to sort out first.'

THE END

Continue to the next page for an extract of

Driven

to

Revenge

A Horror/Fantasy Novel

PROLOGUE

What the hell was wrong with the guy? Did he think he owned the whole bloody road or something?

It was slowly turning out to be one of those awfully bad weeks that you could just do without in all honesty. Eddie Lawson was thirty-eight years old and a single guy, having been divorced seven years earlier, with his wife having finally had enough of his Jekyll and Hyde mood swings once and for all.

Fortunately, there had been no children involved and his ex-wife had long since moved on, having started a new life altogether. This had ended up with her remarrying some other poor sod, just over two years ago, and Eddie was more than pleased with that particular development, as it well and truly kept her off his back.

*

Eddie had dark hair, his face managed to maintain a pretty solemn expression by and large, and his eyes were a clear emerald green, that glistened in the sunlight, as it blasted through the windscreen onto his recently tanned facial features. He could tend to be quite hard and ruthless at times and yet as gentle as a kitten during others. His ex-wife had called him an unstable, dangerous man, especially whenever he sat behind the steering wheel of a car. However, from his point of view, that had been her being a little paranoid at times. It had also been one of her many ways to try and get even with him, especially whenever she became upset, which in his mind had tended to be more often than not.

Right now, his arms felt incredibly stiff in places and a little bit numb from where he'd fought hard to maintain control of his vehicle during an incident that had literally occurred just a few moments ago.

Eddie was still extremely angry with the stupid idiot of a driver in the black BMW.

*

It had all started with the guy speeding up behind him, driving as close as he could to Eddie's back bumper and flashing him all the time. He'd obviously expected him to pull over into the middle lane so that he could overtake. The car must have had some sort of high performance, turbo engine under its bonnet because Eddie could hear how loud it was outside. This was despite having all of his windows closed at the time, although it was not something that bothered him particularly, not at first.

Fortunately, Eddie had been in quite a mild-mannered mood for a change, but as he'd looked around, he'd realised that he had no other option than to continue driving in the fast lane. He'd already been travelling at eighty-nine miles an hour according to his speedometer. This effectively placed him nineteen miles an hour over the legal speed limit for the motorway, plus there'd been a great many cars also careering along at excessive speeds beside him in the middle lane. Where the hell had that twat behind him expected him to go while he'd been boxed in like that? He wondered.

Later, when a gap had finally appeared, Eddie who'd seriously started to lose his cool at that point, deliberately eased across to the middle lane very slowly. His idea was to make the BMW driver wait just a little longer than he wanted. Glancing up and taking a quick look in the rear-view mirror, he noted that the other driver obviously had other ideas at that stage, because he'd suddenly accelerated forward in a futile attempt to squeeze his car into the small opening that had just began to open up, but which was obviously not wide enough for him to pass into just yet. Eddie had foreseen what the madman was about to do at the time, having already spotted him bearing down on him as he'd studied his movements once again in the rear-view mirror. With a tight grip on his steering wheel, Eddie had prepared himself for the impact he knew was about to follow to the back end of his vehicle. Sure enough, the sound of metal against metal had resounded in his ears and he'd watched in total disbelief as the maniac in the BMW still continued with his attempt to squeeze past on the right-hand side. Eddie had tried to manoeuvre his car as fast as he could into the middle lane before the guy caused any further damage, yet sparks now flew in every direction as the driver's side of the other vehicle made contact with the metal barrier that formed the central reservation. This took most of the pressure as the BMW buffeted against it a couple of times, while it waited patiently for an ideal opportunity to tear as much of the bodywork from the hostile vehicle as it could. Eddie could feel the threatening force of the other car as it drew level with him and the two vehicles finally came together. Then, within the space of only a few seconds, he was simply cast aside with ease, as the heavier of the two vehicles ploughed mercifully through.

This took Eddie's right hand side wing mirror with it and flung it up into the air. There was a screech of radial tyres and a distinct smell of burning rubber as the BMW shot off at speed with the driver sticking his middle finger up in the air just to rub salt into the wound.

Rather surprisingly, Eddie took the whole thing quite calmly, turned the steering wheel to the left and slowly applying the brakes, while being sensible enough to make sure that there was plenty of room for any trailing vehicles to avoid disappearing up his arse in the process, as he headed into the slow lane and eventually pulled over onto the hard shoulder before finally coming to a halt. He fully understood just how lucky he'd been as his car could easily have spun across the lanes and been engulfed by the oncoming traffic. However, that had not been the case, and he immediately yanked on the handbrake, placed the gear stick into neutral and then reached out and turned the key in order to turn off the engine.

Taking a few deep breaths before stepping out of the car to assess the damage that had been done, Eddie was immediately made aware of the amount of danger he was in as an articulated lorry passed extremely close by on his right-hand side, which was far too close for comfort. The trailing wind was incredibly strong and it automatically swept his jacket up around his shoulders, much to his growing annoyance. Just as he was smoothing it down against his sides, his eyes suddenly caught sight of some sort of commotion going on about thirty yards behind him in the slow lane of the oncoming traffic, and having made out what was actually occurring, he braced himself for what he hoped was not about to happen.

*

It appeared that the driver had fallen asleep at the wheel, but having woken to the sensation of the car lurching forward and staggering across the carriageway, she struggled with all her might to bring the vehicle back onto an even keel, but sadly it was to no avail.

'No!' screamed Eddie as he saw the dreaded object speeding towards him amidst a column of dust and smoke which spewed forth from a combination of the roads dusty surface and the cars brake pads, which were completely jammed in the locked position.

A split second later, a gaping wound opened up in Eddie's chest, just before he was flung into the air only to find himself landing directly in front of the wheels of another huge lorry as it steamed past the incident with the driver having reacted far too late to do anything about it. Eddie died instantly as his skull was simply crushed to a pulp beneath the heavy double set of wheels that squashed his brain just as if a person had trodden accidentally on a snail. This produced a familiar sound too, as the squelching was pretty loud and audible as it echoed all around.

*

Jane Turner could only gaze in absolute horror as she had no other option than to stare straight ahead as it all unfolded before her eyes. She witnessed Eddie die a horrendous death and was herself hurtled against the protruding steering wheel, as a split second later, her car became one with Eddie's red Rover. She was instantly blinded by the extreme brightness emitted from the blast of the explosion as the engine was blown completely free of its mountings, leaving a huge billowing cloud of smoke trailing behind it as a result. Jane felt intense pain instantaneously shooting up her sides as her legs were forced up at a rather unusual angle. The poor woman screamed in agony and the fear of dying began to settle into her mind as the acrid smell of petrol fumes started to flood the inside of the car. The realisation that she was completely trapped and unable to move in any way, was worse than anything she'd ever imagined possible. Dampness seeped through her clothing in quite a few places and the amount she could feel against her skin told her that she was losing an awful lot of blood, plus everything seemed to be happening in slow motion, which only served to drag out the situation even further.

A huge explosion followed just seconds later, enveloping both vehicles in an enormous ball of flame which was so intense that Jane's remains were finally identified from a copy of her dental records just two days later, once any chance of recovery was possible.

CHAPTER 1

He had been enjoying himself, seemingly without a care in the world, although now it had become a bit of a regular habit. It was great to have a public house so near to the office, especially one that catered for every eventuality and was both warm and friendly inside.

Ted Reynolds was fairly well known amongst the locals. He was a man in his mid-forties and one of those who'd drawn the short straw, as he was balding and wore thick rimmed glasses, which was something that he'd never felt all that comfortable about, since being prescribed them four years earlier. Admittedly, he wasn't much to look at, especially when compared to the Tom Cruise types, but he was certainly seen as a very charming and charismatic person and great fun to be around. Ted was one of those people who had the ability to tell stories that could make your hair curl, provided you had any, and his awful jokes were definitely second to none.

The White Hart public house was decked out in the usual comfy-feely way, as were many such going concerns of a similar ilk, with its old treadle type sewing machine tables containing heavy wrought iron bases with highly polished, dark wooden tops that were easy to clean and as tough as old boots. The wallpaper was a passable shade of green, which according to designer legend, evidently created a nice calming atmosphere. This in respect; supposedly reduced the amount of fights that sometimes broke out amongst the punters in some of the rougher drinking establishments, and The White Hart had certainly not escaped its fair share over the years.

Added lighting with lower wattage bulbs that were cheaper to run and allegedly good for the environment, gave the place a certain dash of gentle ambience and the final touches included hordes of plastic flowers that were never likely to have been to everybody's taste, but still happened to be draped from every available nook and cranny anyway. As things went, business was fairly good on most days, and the place attracted all types of people as it catered for both young and old alike. Over a set period of time, Ted and a few of his work colleagues had gradually formed a group of regular drinking partners, which consisted of some of the employees from the neighbouring manufacturing company located just three buildings away from the pub. The numbers had also risen due to an influx of a few of the locals from the council estate situated just across the road, who'd turned out to be a mad bunch of crazy people, that could certainly hold their beer on the majority of occasions.

This particular evening had been much the same as any other, with Wally arriving late, as always, and asking John the landlord for his usual, the moment he'd said his hello's and reached the bar. What he'd ordered was basically a drink made up from Angostura Bitters, Tomato Juice, a raw egg and last but not least, John's own secret ingredient, which no one had managed to suss out yet. Just like clockwork, Wally would take the glass, instantly throw his head back and swallow the lot in three successive gulps before rushing into the toilet where he'd immediately puke the whole lot up again. This was, and always had been, his ritual for many years, and whenever someone unfamiliar arrived and asked the question, Wally automatically claimed that this tended to clear his stomach out in order to make way for a decent nights drinking ahead, much to the despair of the regulars sitting around just waiting for those words to leave his mouth yet again. Everyone thought the guy was completely off his head, but then again, that was exactly how he'd come to be nicknamed 'Wally' in the first place.

Ted got up, walked across the room and placed a total of thirty pence in the one-armed bandit, which had sat over in the far corner of the pub for as long as he could remember. This amount was the absolute limit that he'd set, in the belief that if he won, he was ahead, and if he lost, then thirty pence would have been no great loss in the great scheme of life in general. He recalled having walked into The Queen Adelaide pub in Shepherds Bush once, many years ago, and having carried out exactly the same technique. Yet after careful insertion of his third and last remaining ten pence piece before playing the bet, lady luck must have been smiling down on him on that occasion as he'd instantly hit the jackpot and become totally embarrassed by the whole thing, as his winnings more than happily poured forth, making enough noise to wake the dead. Gazing around, knowing that he would have drawn so much attention to himself, Ted suddenly found himself being stared at by many of the locals who'd obviously been feeding the damned machine for weeks on end, only to find a total stranger come in off the street and walk away with the top prize of twenty pounds in coins. Ted had also had a few smaller wins on other occasions but had categorically made it a firm rule never to pump any of it back into the ravenous, money hungry machines; that were always ready and waiting to do their worst. It only took a little bit of common sense to understand that the money you put back in would eventually find its way into someone else's pocket, with this someone usually being the landlord, who'd more than happily take their share, albeit they'd still have to pay out what they owed to the rental company who'd be pushing to install more machines or seeking to update the existing ones wherever possible, which again would somehow be linked to an increase in profits.

As he sat with the regular crowd dotted around him, the conversation taking place was essentially geared around their usual range of topics. These generally included the previous night's football results, how each of their teams were doing in the relevant leagues, a no-holds barred show on the television about prostitution and also covered a general discussion about how crappy some of the other programmes had been. As he did so often on a regular basis, Ted reached deep into his pockets and organised his round, and after downing his fourth pint of lager just fifteen minutes later, one of his colleagues stood up just as the bell sounded for last orders and fetched them all another drink for the road.

'Come on you horrible lot!' John the landlord shouted as he and his staff began the laborious task of clearing up, collecting the empty glasses and crisp packets. This was expertly carried out just like a full army manoeuvre as each member of staff had their own specific tasks to concentrate on each night. This also included turning out the remnant dog ends from the ashtrays and giving the tabletops a fleeting glimpse of water from a slightly dampened cloth, which in turn meant that the pub was always kept reasonably clean and up to an acceptable standard, which was another reason why the punters chose to return time after time.

Having waved farewell to everyone, Ted was the first to leave and casually weaved his way along the pavement towards his car, parked in his usual parking place at the back of the pub. The 1995 N registration Vauxhall Calibra in nautilus blue contained all the trimmings he required; electric windows, a sunroof, alloy wheel trims and an immobiliser. This was considered to be Ted's pride and joy, although It still cost him quite a bit every month, due to the terms of the financial agreement that he'd hurriedly taken on, after he'd part exchanged his old car fourteen months earlier. Having carried out this exact same routine, having left the pub on a fairly regular basis over the past few years, Ted was quite used to ignoring the fact that his alcohol consumption had now placed him well over the legal limit allowed for driving a vehicle whilst under the influence of intoxicating substances. Having pulled out of the car park and blended in with the rest of the traffic travelling this usually quiet street, Ted suddenly realised that he hadn't yet put his lights on. This certainly wasn't the first time and he sure as hell didn't think it would be the last. He had of course done this many times in the past on quite a few other instances, and was pretty thankful that the police hadn't been around to spot him doing it yet again. As he turned the next corner, he happily joined the traffic in the high street, and noticed that signs were being put in place by workmen wearing high visibility jackets in preparation for some road works that were obviously about to take place fairly soon. That would at least explain why so many of the side roads appeared to be a little bit busier tonight. After leaving the centre of town, the road had eventually petered out and the darkness of the countryside slowly began to spread itself out around him. Having taken in a good deal of fresh air through the open window on his right-hand side, Ted could feel that his senses had dulled a little and started to feel very tired all of a sudden, as large expanses of open fields sped past with the views he was currently obtaining via the windows on each side of the car. As he rounded the next bend however, he suddenly received the fright of his life as the headlights of a huge oncoming articulated lorry lit up the whole expanse of road along with all the surroundings which cast a whole host of shadows reaching this way and that. It was all very confusing at that particular moment and the sound of the lorry driver, who had his hand jammed firmly on the horn, echoed all around. It was a clear enough warning, which basically told him to either get out of the middle of the road as fast as he could, or become mashed up and part of the tarmac; the choice was his. Although his reflexes were much slower than usual, due to his intake of too much alcohol, Ted just managed to pull over in the nick of time. His heart was almost in his mouth at that point and he immediately felt the adrenaline rising within his body, as the two vehicles passed by each other with only a fraction of an inch separating the gap that stood between them. After the lorry had completely disappeared from sight, having already woken most of the countryside up, Ted gazed into his rear-view mirror and within a few fleeting seconds, dead calm seemed to return and order once again prevailed. The remainder of the drive home was completed without any further problems of any kind and Ted somehow managed to stay wide awake and fully alert at the wheel for the duration of the journey. Fifteen minutes later the man slumped still half-dressed onto his bed, knowing only too well that he was extremely lucky to be alive, this time around at least.

*

The coming of day had turned the western sky into a hotchpotch of many colours during the last few mornings, as was fitting for that time of the year, and it was currently in the process of altering from a dusky red into a murky pale blue colour. Amanda Day hated the morning rush at the best of times. It was always so manic at this hour of the day as she tried with great effort to get her older child, David to school on time. This was a task that was made even harder due to the fact that the child was always so slow when it came to getting dressed. He was such a plodder in the mornings, always had been and she had no doubt about guessing that he always would be. What also didn't help the cause a great deal; was that four-year-old Tony, the younger of the two boys, was just as much of a handful and consequently behaved like a complete monster most of the time. Amanda's husband, Martin invariably made sure that he took her in a cup of tea in the mornings before heading off to work, and would always kiss her lightly on the forehead before creeping down the stairs to put on his coat and pick up his rucksack prior to leaving the house, carefully closing the door with his keys rather than letting it slam shut, as it was prone to do on the odd occasion, for some reason best known to itself. The stairs were always quite a feat and something that Indiana Jones would more than likely find a bit of a challenge, as he had to try to avoid all of the squeaky sections of the staircase, so as not to wake the children before leaving the house to catch his train to work. This didn't always go quite according to plan however, because every so often he'd be greeted by

David, who sometimes woke up far too early for his own good, and then complained that he was terribly tired in the evening time. During such instances, Martin would tend to find him sitting around playing with his toys or be drawing or making some kind of ungodly creation in the dining room. Amanda was usually just about conscious enough to emit a grunt of acknowledgement, as she battled internally against the temptation that was always trying to force her to go back to sleep again as well as the constant reminders being emitted by her alarm clock every now and again. However, some form of miracle always seemed to occur, as his wife would eventually manage to rise up from the comfort and safety of the duvet and get herself washed and dressed as part of the daily routine that so needed to happen. Later, with both the children having already had their breakfast shovelled down their throats in what seemed like a matter of minutes, they were finally sitting comfortably in the rear of the family car. Tony was now firmly secured in his toddler seat attempting to pull the head off his toy Postman Pat, and David had climbed in and strapped himself tightly into his grey plastic booster seat, which he was always so adamant about doing on his own, without any help from an adult. Suddenly, for the first time in ages, Amanda realised that the noise level was actually quite tolerable for a change as she started the car, set off down the road and passed by her best friend's house, which was set slightly back from the road, and partially hidden behind a row of fir trees, which provided screening to a certain extent, but evidently needed regular pruning, otherwise they'd have grown completely wild.

*

Daniel Grant was quite relaxed as he sat and waited for the lights to change. There was only one part of the journey that he really disliked, and that was at a junction with a small crossroads whose traffic lights only ever let about three cars through at any one time. It was rumoured that a mini-roundabout was going to be built there sometime in the future, but Daniel was a realist and had already made up his mind that he would only believe it when he saw it for himself as he continued on and passed a series of shops that flanked the road on both sides. He'd worked at his existing company as a maintenance engineer for a whole seven years now, and was generally quite settled and fairly happy with what he did for a living. During that time, he'd also seen the firm increase in size from six engineers, who used to cover the south of the country, to a team that now consisted of twenty-seven engineers in total. Three of the latest engineers that had been taken on in recent months were essentially highly competent women, and certainly a force to be reckoned with, from what they'd seen so far. Taking this number and adding it to the amount of managers, administration staff and not forgetting the stock controller that had long since been employed to keep an eye on the stores. The total number of staff in his office had since increased to thirty-four, and still appeared to be rising on a monthly basis, which was very good news indeed as far as he and the rest of the company were concerned. The head office based in the north of the country was already double the size of the one he worked from, but they did also cover the whole of Scotland and Ireland to be fair.

Daniel usually left the house early in order to skip around the M25 motorway before it became too clogged up with the regular rush hour traffic, as he hated the constant starting and stopping that came as part and parcel of that particular section of the overcrowded motorway during that part of the day. This usually allowed him to have a fairly safe ride in, and once he'd arrived, he generally found that he could sit and have his breakfast in absolute peace and quiet with the added bonus of being able to clear up any of what he deemed to be, minor tasks still hanging around, which often wasted so much of his precious time first thing in the morning. In addition to getting in so early, this also meant that he also had the whole place to himself and basically had the run of the office and all of its facilities before it turned into a complete and utter mad house. The only exception to this rule was on Fridays, when he and a colleague called Keith Reynolds would meet for an early morning swim and simply have a chance to catch up with each other and spend a little bit of time talking about the world at large, while trying their best to solve a few of the issues that currently frequented the television and newspapers. This generally took place in the local leisure centre's sauna, which they'd both agreed, was a fantastic way to relax and clear away their troubles once a week, especially before starting a day of hard graft, which usually concerned quite a bit of driving, as the area they covered was fairly substantial, when compared against a map of the UK. They'd often stop for a leisurely breakfast of tea and toast by the poolside, whilst scanning the wide selection of newspapers that were readily available to all of the early morning customers. Once they'd both gotten fully dressed, Daniel and Keith were always amazed at how good they felt as soon as the electric doors whooshed open and the fresh air hit them as they left the leisure complex together, just before heading off for their company cars which were usually parked next to each other in the impressively large car park, which even contained an additional overflow area at the back. Once inside their vehicles, it would then become a race to see who could be the first to reach the office in the quickest time via the twisting and turning trails of the backstreets that they already knew so well.

Daniel was really looking forward to having a break in three weeks' time, when he and his beautiful fiancé would happily be taking a holiday for a whole two weeks in the sunny climes of Greece, and this was what was uttermost on his mind as he raced along with Keith's car already taking the next bend in front of him.

ABOUT THE AUTHOR

Stephen Harding has written some of the most exciting books you will ever read. Unique, stimulating, ingenious, dark, mind-blowing, spine-tingling and twisted are words that would best be linked to his creations.

In 2008 his short play 'My Bench' won third prize in the Kingston Readers Festival before being published. Inspired by Stephen King's 'On Writing', he decided to publish his first novel 'Janus the Arrival' in 2013, having cut out the filler that bores so many readers. The sequel 'Janus the Offspring' followed in 2014 with the third part of the trilogy 'Janus the Sandlings' coming later that same year. 'Driven to Revenge' a horror/fantasy was released in 2016 with a crime thriller 'Twice Bad' featuring Detective Liberty Rock in 2017 with the sequel 'ISO Killer' released in 2019.

He dislikes stories where you can always guess what happens next, so tends to twist the plot in order to shake up the reader by calling on his love of books, films to gain new ideas. Stephen is passionate about encouraging others to read and write. He currently lives in London with his wife and has drawn on good and bad encounters in the business world and life in general. He hopes you enjoy his works as well as he enjoys creating them.

For further information about Stephen Harding, please visit:

- www.amazon.com/author/stephen.harding
- Facebook: Novels by Stephen Harding
- https://twitter.com/LexxyJanus

or contact him on: s.hardingnovels@gmail.com

Printed in Great Britain
by Amazon